PIECES

AND *Me*

THE STUFF THAT WAKES ME UP AT NIGHT

BY EMILY (E) CLAUDETTE FREEMAN

PIECES. AND. ME
The Stuff That Wakes Me Up At Night
E. Claudette Freeman

Library of Congress Control Number: 2016921554
ISBN 10: 0988896982
ISBN 13: 978-0-9888969-8-7

Pecan Tree Publishing
Printed in the United States of America
Hollywood, FL.

PECAN TREE PUBLISHING

Hollywood, Fl.
www.pecantreebooks.com

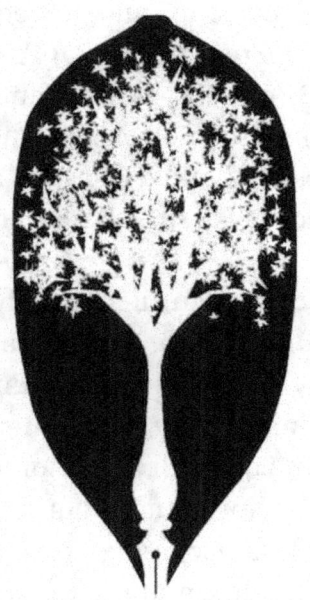

New Voices | New Styles | New Vision

TO US Y'ALL...

This book is dedicated to Isaiah Langston-Michael Freeman, who loves me, challenges me, excites me, enrages me, makes me think – has been my weakness and my strength. My life was made so much more interesting from the moment I called you son. You are my greatest blessing.

This book is dedicated to my mom, Annie Thomas, because she is my mom and praise God, a cancer survivor. I love you.

This book is dedicated to Tatiana Freeman, Camisha Freeman, Douglas T. Freeman, Sr., DJ Freeman, Kennedi Freeman, Tammy Norton, RJ Scriven, and Tamijah Scriven (my buddy for life), Annie Bowens, Antinori Harris, Deanna Harris, Deion McNeal, Claudia Chastain and Cailin Chastain. And to my godchildren Larenna Barias and her heart – Amir; and Austin Smith.

This book is dedicated to all my family that began from the warmth of Pelham, Georgia or whose branches somehow lead there. For my dad, Douglas Charles Freeman, and my grandparents who I still miss dearly, and sometimes profoundly - James Thomas, Sr., Lucille Bryant Thomas; and Luiza and Walker Freeman. For my aunts and uncles who have transitioned Mamie and Isaac Cochran, Sr., Nathaniel Thomas, James Thomas, Jr.(Shorty); Addie and I.C. Cochran; and others whose generational blood and roots we hailed from and grew with – Godspeed.

And for all of you from around the way - here are our lives, our stories, our tomorrows.

ACKNOWLEDGMENTS

Where would I be without the love, grace, mercy, wisdom and blessings of my Lord and Savior. Through doubts, misguided steps, false pretenses, miles of mouths full of discouragement, you have given me understanding and the strength to stand up, and not lay down my dreams. Your power and your love is more than I deserve and all that I will ever need.

Roland Athouris, words could never express the gratitude I hold for you. You didn't have to take on my vision. I never really understood why you did. But 20 years ago, you did more than design a cover and lay out a book for a new friend and first time author. You decided to publish that book; and sow into my vision powerfully. May God, bless you one hundredfold for your kindness and your faith in my gift.

Thank you for your impact Bhetty Waldron, Vinnette Carroll, Ntozake Shange, Tina McElroy Ansa, Zora Neale Hurston and James Baldwin.

To each of you that push me to write, that ask what I have written, that ask when is the next project – thank you, thank you, thank you.

INTRODUCTION

What is it about old people that make them such natural story tellers? And is that thing, also what makes small town people such great story tellers? And is it possible that as an African-American woman, no matter where I am, if there are people like me with similar heritages and backgrounds, there will always be great story tellers, and wondrous stories to be told? That's what it is all about. Heritage through the memories of those who can still recall. The details sometimes dressed up in more clever clothing. The people often transposed to fit the occasion. The timing off just a little because the internal clock itself needs re-winding.

Through the speak-easies of wooden Georgia porches, I have learned so many things. Amazingly they were never really things I paid any attention to then. You figure your great aunt is basically telling lies to keep company laughing, until you hear other people disclosing little bits of knowledge. You never really know how these porch stories and quick witted tales impressed you, until you find yourself engaged in a swapping of tales with someone else. And then suddenly, it's like you're sitting under the tree or on that porch, and with every story you're trying to get "one up" on the competition.

Or there are other things . . . like the way you always know what terms like knee-baby, ice box, and cooling shed mean; although you never say anything, because, well then people know you know. Or how about when you find yourself talking about the best way to slaughter a hog with someone, who also has knowledge of this; but you suddenly grow quiet when someone else walks into the room. Or how about when you cook a pot of white acre peas and get pissed off, because although you did a good job, they just are not tasting like they did at home, or when aunt Mae cooked them. We've been impressed upon.

Zora Neale Hurston had a way of making Joe Clark's front porch dance for me. Through the language of the towns people so vividly laid out on the pages before me, I could taste their sorrow, feel the crumbling hearts of women whose husbands spared a few moments at the general store to tell of their mis-doings, their reality was a film that I wanted to be a part of. A movie about us that would never make the box office, because in its simplicity, the language was considered stupid and hard to read, rather than appreciated for its personality and life. To celebrate our different tongues, different voices, different highs and lows is what a story properly carried out should do.

Bringing the language of my hometown . . . words cut to the quick . . . sounds dismissed for their un-unnecessariness . . . flairs and rises at the most inopportune time, to life is fun. I am re-visiting a side of me that I thought gone. The curious girl who questioned why I questioned everything. The simple girl who appreciated the simple pleasures of insignificant material things and the importance of powerful relationships. The professional woman who thought she wanted to be aggressive, yet deep inside knows all she wants to do is not have to put on make-up and heels for yet another meeting.

I am as barefoot and at home now as I could ever be. Because I have truly come to know, that the stories of life will unfold as I go, and therefore I will always have a porch on which to re-collect them; even if the wood is only in my mind. And the impression is only in my heart.

Emily Claudette Freeman

Contents

PIECES

And *Me*

THE STUFF THAT WAKES ME UP AT NIGHT

EMILY (E) CLAUDETTE FREEMAN

I Held Them In My Arms

Miss James still cooked huge pots of everything on holidays. The mass cooking would be alright if she was doing all that dicing, slicing, mincing, chopping and baking for a whole bunch of people, but she wasn't. Hard times had kept her daughters and grandkids from coming home for the holidays for almost three years. But this year, she kept telling everybody in the neighborhood, she felt like a family was going to be together.

In an old neighborhood like the predominantly Black, middle to older age Bevel Lakes everybody pretty much knows a little about everybody else. Most of the families here settled in when their oldest child was the only child. So, we've seen numerous graduations, weddings and yes, funerals. Even in a time where teenage mothers and thirty-something-year old grandmothers would rather curse you out for correcting their child than appreciating the fact that someone was looking out for them, we are still a pretty, tight-knit neighborhood – especially our little cul-de-sac.

In our pocket is Miss James, me – Shay Anthony (I don't know what my mom was thinking either – Shay, it's a sound not a name), Mr. and Mrs. Roberts, Carol Richards and her two sons, and Mr. Matthews. I am the baby home owner inheriting the house from my parents. Miss James was my first baby sitter. She has two daughters - Kathy and Charlene; both are in Detroit, and together they have eight kids. The two of them used to help their mother watch neighborhood kids and make sure the latch key kids got home when they were supposed to and had something hot to eat – until their parents arrived.

Kathy moved to Detroit when her husband took a job there. Charlene followed to help Kathy take care of her two kids. Soon after, she herself got married, had three kids and got divorced a month before she discovered number four was waiting in the wings. When Kathy's husband was killed in a car accident, Miss

James flew up to help her pull things together and to re-assure her daughters that to would pass. She often told me that she worried about Kathy more, even though she was the oldest, she didn't have Charlene's faith or resilience. Charlene didn't know how to give up or when to give in.

I kind of missed having the two of them around. I missed having my parents too. Miss James has been good for me in that regard. We talk to each other a lot and at her daughters' requests I make sure she's looked out for properly. And I regularly keep them updated on her doctor's visits, financial situation and her overall spirit. She has an amazing spirit. She has an amazing faith. It's like nothing I have ever seen before.

I called Charlene Thanksgiving morning, about 5, like I always do. She didn't answer. I called Kathy shortly thereafter figuring that they had combined residences for the cold and hard winter. Charlene had been having problems keeping up her utility bills, so we talked about them moving in together to get through the rough times. Kathy didn't answer either, but rather than worry, I realized that they were probably still fast asleep and promised myself I would call back later. I chuckled, realizing Miss James had probably told them about how she felt like a family was going to be together and somehow, they had figured out a way to get everyone back to Miami for her holiday cooking.

Miss James and I made the final touches on the turkey and I nibbled on the ham, as she flipped through the channels trying to find part of the Macy's Thanksgiving Day parade. When I was little, the whole neighborhood would gather at my house or Miss James' and watch the parade with card tables lined up along one wall. The tables held a breakfast pot luck that rivaled the best restaurants and could feed an army. We would eat and give commentary, waiting until the very end to see Snoopy go floating by. Then the kids would try to duplicate the parade action, marching around the cul-de-sac with an enormous amount of racket.

"Looka there Shay, they still got Snoopy. Children these days don't know nothing 'bout no Snoopy. Snoopy Shag maybe."

Her laughter filled the air; and I couldn't help but laugh too, knowing she really went . . . Snoop Dogg, yet another notorious rapper that my godchildren and her grandchildren wanted to be. Our laughter was interrupted by a special news report. Our Thanksgiving was interrupted by the thought of giving thanks in spite of.

"Lord, child I'm gone start praying now. Some poor people gone have a hard time this holiday."

And that's what she did . . . started praying. And crying. And praying. I sat in horror. The second they showed the apartment building in flames I knew it was the one that Kathy lived in. The reporter herself was crying, her report almost unclear through the tears and emotion. A fire in two units on the fourth floor totally engulfed both apartments and seriously damaged six others on the fourth, fifth and third floors. Miss James began crying out to the Lord. The loudest, most pained cried I had ever heard. As her voice got louder I felt my stomach folding inward like nothing I'd ever experienced.

Most of the apartments were vacant. But the tiny bodies on one of the stretchers that a camera man focused in on told me at least one of the apartments wasn't. The fire apparently started when a gas or kerosene lamp was knocked over. The flames became short explosions when they caught the aura of gas from the stove. Eight kids and three adults were killed, two others seriously injured. The names were being withheld until the families could be notified. Miss James yelled out "JESUS", then fainted.

I panicked. The camera flashed across the crowd and suddenly there was Charlene. The police holding her back, the look on her face as they spoke to her, confirming what Miss James already knew. The kids and Kathy were dead. I ran to the front door and started screaming, realizing Miss James was lying on the floor and her family was gone. Carol and Jose pulled me back inside.

"We saw it Shay, we saw. Where's Mama James?" I pointed to her unconscious body on the floor. What was going to happen now?

An hour passed before the phone finally rang. Charlene tried to relay the news, but could only sob. A neighbor of hers confirmed the worst news I have ever had to share. She said she worked for social services and could help us make any arrangements.

"I saw them carrying bodies out on a stretcher . . . " I felt the words push through the fog in my mind.

"We think it was Charlene's youngest and Kathy's two youngest. But we're not sure. I don't know really how to say this . . . " This woman I didn't know before this call, sobbed, like the pain in Charlene's soul was now her own.

"Say it somehow, please. I don't want her to see on the news like I just did. What is it?" I already knew, perhaps, I thought – I'm wrong. What she said literally knocked the very life out of me and I felt myself falling. Then I felt Josh catch me.

"Basically, all they got to make identification from is bones and pieces of clothes. The three little ones died of smoke inhalation. Seems somebody tried to get them far enough away to go back and get the others. There really is nothing to ship to you." All I heard then was a wail, a wail that must have even brought the angels to tears. She yelled for someone to hold her, just hold her.

Slobbering and blubbering, I was fighting off every word I heard her say. As though fighting it would make it any better. "Nothing . . . no bodies, no bodies. . . . "

Miss James awakened from her time before the Lord to hear my ramblings to Charlene's neighbor.

"Shay you tell her I said, whatever is there comes here. . . . " The power in her voice shook me, clearly, she didn't hear enough of the conversation.

"But Mama James, she says there's. . . . " Her small, brown hand raised in determination, slapped whatever I thought I was going to say back down my throat.

"Listen to me girl. I told you my family was going to be together for the holiday this year and we are. I got to bring my babies home. I shoulda been brought my babies home. You tell her, whatever is there comes here and it comes now."

I couldn't even begin to understand the strength through anger and forgiveness that must have been filling Miss James at this moment. I couldn't even imagine what it must have done to her to realize as she watched the building in flames that a large part of her bloodline had been ripped from her bosom.

"Ma'am. You still there?" The neighbor's voice stirred me back to the original conversation.

"Yes, I'm here. I'm sorry. Did you hear what she said?"

"Yes, I did. I'll do whatever I can for you. You should know something else." A deep breath escaped through the phone.

"What's that?"

"Charlene, the last baby . . . she tore away from the police and got to the stretcher. She held the three little ones in her arms, when they were trying to . . . The last baby, cried for just a few seconds then he died in her arms. Right, in her arms. She's not doing well. I'm not sure she really knows. . . . " Her tears spoke the things that words weren't designed to describe.

"Oh, my God. My God. May I have your number? I guess, I guess we'll need to touch basis and get through this."

She gave me all her available numbers and I struggled to write them down legibly. I watched my hands trembling fiercely. This was going to be a day that would not end. I knew it. And the work of picking up and pulling together pieces began. Carol got Charlene on a flight out the next morning. The coroner's office reported that what was left of the deceased, beyond the three little ones, would be sent home in one box. Carol insisted that they be shipped individually, with the proper names according to dental records. As hard as it would be, she knew Mama James would want them all to get their due respect. They also told her, the third adult killed was Victor Ramings, Charlene's ex-husband. The neighbor later told us, he had come by to catch up his child support payments and got stuck when his car wouldn't start. He fell asleep on the couch waiting for Charlene to come home.

Mama James busied herself in the kitchen. She frosted the chocolate cake, reminding me that it was Kathy's favorite. Carol set the table for dinner and sent her son to gather everybody on the street. It was strange, everybody trickled in, but the strength in the room was from Miss. James.

"We not gone do no whole lotta crying and carrying on. Naw, this ain't the way I wanted my family home, but it is the Lord's will and somehow. . . . " The tears poured into her shaking palms. "Somehow the Lord gone get some glory and I'm awfully mad at Him right now, but He gone get some glory."

Quietly, Carol led her back to the bedroom. Together, the rest of the neighborhood talked about how we could help her get through this. All I could think about was Charlene. Hours alone on a flight, knowing that just a few short feet away are the bodies of your only sister, your children and the man you said you knew you were meant to be with no matter what. Hours alone on a flight, remembering the feeling of three little bodies in your arms and knowing you will never lose the sound of that baby's last cries. I prayed for her. I prayed that the resilience she was known for her would not leave her now.

Charlene becoming a mother was a major coupe. She was always a tom-boy and birthing babies was the farthest thing from her. We, Miss James and I, laughed for the longest time when she got pregnant the first time. But she was an awesome mother. The last time Kathy, Charlene and the kids were home we went to see some horror movie and six little people started screaming at one time. And they all went in one direction – to Charlene's lap. She held them all in her arms for the rest of the movie. There was no distinction between her kids and Kathy's kids and it was the same way for Kathy. It was always the children need – and "the children" meant them all. Now that whole connection was gone for her.

"Carol, Shay, Jeannie." Miss James called from the bedroom. "I got to make sure Charlene gon' be all right. I'm not quite sure how to do that. You know she get awfully quiet when things bother her. But she don't need to close up now. If all she does is cry out to the Lord – she don't need to close up."

Carol nodded acknowledging Miss James' concern. Mrs. Rodgers did likewise. "Mama James," said Carol, "Charlene can stay at my house; it might be easier than seeing everything around here. Until she's ready to face it you know."

"I believe Katey, the church has a special counselor for tragic situations like this. Let me call Pastor Bly's office. Sometimes it's easier to let go with folks that don't know you." Miss James gave Mrs. Rodgers an approval nod, and she stepped away from the room and set about making necessary calls.

"Carol, why don't you let Charlene stay with Shay. That way you don't have to inconvenience your boys. Anyhow, Charlene might talk it through with Shay."

Carol turned to face me, her look urging me to let Miss James know that her idea would be fine. I inhaled deeply, hoping to gain the air of faith she was breathing into the space. "Yes ma'am, she can stay with me. I'll do what I can."

Days passed and Charlene said nothing. We had hoped that the funeral would create a breakthrough for her; but it didn't. It was one of the hardest funerals I have ever attended. And I have buried both my parents, which for an only child is a devastating thing. But to see those coffins, eight holding the remains of children who hadn't even seen their 13 birthdays yet was horrible. Miss James was unreal. She was a rock. I watched her take Charlene by the arm and walk her to every one of those coffins, closed as they were, to tell them good-bye. "You close the door baby. The devil gets no joy out of your family's death. You will stand up and tell them your love does not die and that God will hold them from here on out." I swear you could hear her bones rattling from the way her body shook. You could barely see her eyes behind the well of tears that clung to them. But she did it. She did it. The whole service Charlene only said one thing, she calmly touched her mother's hand and through broken words told her, "I had just cut Kathy's hair, she knew you would have a fit. It was really short."

I left for work shortly before nine as normal. Telling Charlene that I would take her out for dinner when I got home. Nine days and she wouldn't even look out the window. Nine days and Miss James would come over and sit with her, cook for her, love her. Charlene would just hold on, but she wouldn't cry. Miss James stopped me as I placed the key into the door and began to turn it. Sullen and worn, she wore the mask of a defeated mother. I held her weakened frame. I knew she was losing yet another child and I couldn't tell her.

"I can't go in there today Shay. I can't do it."

That statement threw me. "She needs you Miss James."

9

"That's the problem. I ain't what she needs, but I'm what she keeps getting. She still thinking it's gone be all right and it can't be 'til she let go. She letting the devil turn her memories into ghosts and that I can't stop. She gon' have to do it herself."

"What happens if she can't?"

"I'm praying that she can. If she doesn't remember nothin' else, she knows that she's loved by God. And God ain't gave us the spirit of fear, but of love, power and a strong mind. You gone to work. Prayerfully by the time you get home – my baby will be on her way back home too."

Charlene used to laugh at me a lot. I had an imaginary friend that didn't like Charlene, so whenever I did something mean and rotten to her I blamed it on Diana. Charlene said I was crazy. Then I developed this love for photography in sixth grade and it blossomed into a full career. I had forgotten about the photos I had taken over the years. I had forgotten about the videotapes of those photos I have. Birthday parties, anniversaries, weddings, the birth of Kathy's third child and Charlene's second, they were days apart. I videotaped both, so that Miss James could see their births for herself when I got back to Miami. I remembered telling Kathy and Charlene that the next time I visited I'd like to see more than the maternity ward.

It all came rushing back as I drove to work and realized that the albums and videotapes were in the living room. Why that suddenly made a difference I didn't know. They had been on the same entertainment center for awhile. Suddenly though, I feared Charlene would find them and it would be too much for her. Still, I couldn't go back home; I had major client meetings and, for some reason, of all mornings, there was a horrendous traffic back-up on Sheets Boulevard in both directions. So, I stayed my course and eventually made it to work.

The thought of Charlene finding the photo archive eventually left and I ended up doing an extra hour and a half at work. When I tried to call, and tell her to be dressed so we could go out and grab a bite, the phone just rang. I figured Miss James or one of the neighbors had finally gotten her out of the house. I gathered my mess and headed home.

Pulling into the drive way, I couldn't help but notice the house was unusually dark. It seemed as though nothing had changed or moved from the way I left it that morning. That worried me. That meant, Charlene still lie in bed staring at the walls. I thought about what Miss James said, about allowing the devil to turn your memories into ghosts. I couldn't let that happened. Turning the key in the door and pushing it open, I could see Charlene decided she couldn't let that happen either. She had indeed found the photographs and the videos. She sat on the couch, crying and laughing, as she watched her child being born. When she turned, and saw me, she fell into tears.

"My baby was so beautiful. I have never seen a child born as pretty as she was. Kathy had beautiful children. We used to laugh about Marky, because he looked so much like his father when he was born – long, dark and real hairy. Kathy used to pray he would outgrow his "monkey" stage. Oh, God Shay. Why them? Shay I couldn't hold them all in my arms, and he just cried. Oh, God, why my babies? Why my babies?"

I held her and called Miss James. Together we walked her back to the house she grew up in to face what she no longer wanted to see. Or so she thought. She thought forgetting the smiles on their faces and the way they cried would make the pain go away faster. It hadn't. She didn't want to see the pictures of she and Kathy hanging and standing all around her mother's house. She couldn't handle the comfort and security of a child clinging to her mother's breast, because her babies could no longer cling to her. But somehow, she found her way through hours of pain and crying to that safe place again.

Days passed before Miss James told me Charlene called from Detroit to say she was catching a late flight out. She was fine. Much against our wishes she chose to go back alone to wrap up lingering things. Miss James said there was an excitement in her voice. There apparently were no more ghosts, but the memories of eight children and a sister who loved each other, cared for each other and made it through hard times and even death together.

"And the devil lost again," so said Miss James.

All About Miss
Chayonne's Porch

Sometimes I get so tired of mama and daddy's complaining; that's why I just tell them I'm going to Jamie Taylor's house now, or I sneak out the window and go up by Miss Chayonne's house. They say Miss Chayonne is a foul-mouthed, raunchy old woman, that ain't got half her sense left. I think she's funny. She knows everything 'bout everybody in this town. One day, I told her, I was going to sit down and write a book about this place and call it, Pelham Blues. She told me she believes I will do just that.

Miss Chayonne, like I said is full of stories, though most folks 'round these parts believe she mostly telling lies, I believe she mostly telling truths and that's why people wish she would just shut up sometimes. She tells me time and time again I should have seen her in her younger days and I wished I could've. I've seen pictures of her, she was beautiful, high yellow skin, with that wavy hair pulled to the back and pinned up with flowers along the side, mascara to make her eyes look real dark and lots of red lipstick. She ain't never been married, says she ain't met a man worth having her yet. I like that, I figure he, whoever I marry, gots to be worth me too.

Lots of folks come 'round Miss Chayonne when they get off work, for a shot of hooch. They sit on the porch and talk loud and long. Normally, less you kin to her, Miss Chayonne run kids off. But every time I come by I brings her a can of snuff and sometimes I come by jes to brush her hair down for her. Of course, we always do that inside cause she don't like folks to see her all natural like that. When I went by there last night, Earl James, Cliff and Mattie Mae was already there, Miss Ann came by a little later.

"Hey Miss Chayonne. I come to bring you that snuff and a loaf of bread like you wanted. Should I put it in the house?"

"You know where it go Sugar. How your people doing?"

"They all right. Daddy got a touch of the flu, he acting like it's the end of the world."

"Men folks just like that chile, they ain't got no better sense. Simple cough have 'em crying."

Earl James took offense to that remark, "Aah, 'cuse me Chayonne. You ought not feed that chile such nonsense. Men feel colds worse than women, cause we ain't use to being sick like y'all is."

Miss Chayonne spit right quick and let him have it. "You damn fool, what kind of foolishness is that?"

"It's a natu'l fact ain't it Cliff," he nudged Cliff awake trying to prove his point.

"Yes, it is. It's a mighty real fact. Hell, everybody know women just gone get sick mo' than men."

"Take yo' sorry behind back to sleep Cliff, you the last one to be tellin' somebody 'bout women." Miss Chayonne leaned forward real slow like in her chair. "If a woman get sick more than a man, it's cause she spen'ng too much time and energy taking care y'all no accounts asses, and yo' pissy-tailed young'uns. If a man act like a man, woman wouldn't have to be both."

"Heh heh, tell the truth Chay!" Now usually Miss Ann just sit and listen, so when I heard her get excited I knew she had to have had a couple of glasses of hooch in her already. "When I was younger, not that I's old now, but years ago, I had me a man. Looked finer than wine and was smoother than cake batter, girl, that man could do it to me good."

"All right Ann, you see that girl here," Miss Chayonne motioned for me to sit down next to her. I laughed at Miss Chayonne protecting me and at the thought of Miss Ann, who wasn't much bigger than a 12-year-old, hunching wit' anybody. Folks say it's been ten years since she combed her hair.

"It's okay Miss Chayonne, some nights I reckon I hear you say worse."

"Sho you do Sugar," said Miss Ann, sashaying out in the courtyard. "This man would come see me, and I'd put on my nylons, my purls, and my sweet perfume that I ordered from the catalog; and we'd hit town. Chile I was wild for the way that man could dance."

Miss Ann got real sad all of a sudden, she stopped dancing, stopped smiling, just plopped down on the porch. Me, I looked up at Miss Chayonne, but she didn't say nothing. I wanted to hear the rest of the story, so I asked her plainly. "Whatever happened to him Miss Ann?"

Miss Chayonne slapped her knee. "Damn! You shouldna asked her that!"

Miss Ann cried just a little bit, "He left a dance one night with this white woman, next thang I hear he in jail for raping her. I ain't heard tale of him since."

"Now I'll be a suck-head mule," Cliff was suddenly wide awake. "When you told that story yesterday, woman, you said the man left a dance and got shot by his wife. You don't know what the hell happen to that man do you?"

"Shut yo' ole drunk ass up, I do knows what happen to him, it ain't none of yo business." I had never seen Miss Ann so upset. "Run in there, Sugar and get me some ice fo' ma drink baby."

"Ann. I knows what happened to that jackass ya know. Why you just don't tell folks the truth, if you gone be telling the story." I heard Miss Chayonne from her kitchen, right before I heard the horn blow. "Hey there Shorty, what's going on?"

Shorty is the evening paper boy. He always brings Miss Chayonne paper right to her hands. Folks say he threw that paper one time so hard he knocked the latch off Miss Chayonne door and it flew open. There she sat on her chamber pot.

16

I mostly think he brings it to her personal so he can get a drink, if she feels like giving him one, 'fore he go out to the country. He didn't tarry long though. But he did visit long enough to tell us all something that just broke Mattie Mae poor heart. I didn't know why.

Miss Chayonne tried to comfort her, I think. "Don't you sit yo stupid butt here and cry. Now you knew full well that man was married and worse than that he couldn't keep his dick in his pants."

Still Mattie Mae was hurting, "I loved that man. Why somebody had to go and kill him? Couldn't they just shoot him a l'il bit?"

"Lord give me strength," Miss Chayonne stood up laughing, "Baby ain't no such thang as shootin' somebody a l'il bit. That's like being pregnant a l'il bit. That damn fool probably got caught laid up wit' some woman and her man loaded his ass wit' buckshot."

"Shonuff," said Earl James.

"Probably just what happened too." Cliff agreed with the others.

Miss Ann did likewise, "Un huh, and from what I hear, he wa'nt 'bout nothin.'"

Mattie Mae head was hung so low, I felt sorry for her. I ain't never been in love, but I figure I'm 14, my time got to be comin' pretty soon. But if being in love gone have me looking pitiful like Mattie Mae, I reckon I keep my love to myself.

Cliff poured his self another drink, "What day that was Shorty say that boy got killed?"

"He say it was Wednesday night," Earl James said pushing his cup towards the bottle being passed on.

Mattie Mae looked confused, "See it couldn't been no woman problem, Ray was wit' me Wednesday night. I swear he was."

Miss Chayonne simply shook her head. "Honey he was wit' you part of the night. Wednesday night was Ray's busy night. He had to comfort you, Betty Mae, cause that's the night her husband go hunting, and he usually go comfort Missy Lee out by Thomasville way too."

"Hush lying Miss Chayonne. Ray loved me. He wouldna slept wit' nobody else the same night he comforted me. That's sho mean spirited o' ya." Mattie Mae was pacing the yard. I don't reckon I'd want anybody to tell me some news like that either.

"Gal, I done tried to tell you time and time again, 'bout that man. But you was a fool and wa'nt listenin'. Let me tell ya somethin' else too, hot ass, if a man love ya he ain't got no business sleepin' with any other woman any time, not jes the night he comfortin' you. Anyhow, you been smellin' behind Pearl and Eddie's boy lately. So, you couldna been too much in love."

I laughed, "Mattie Mae, not the one with the one big eye and the one l'il one. Is it him?"

"Shut up Sugar. He's a sweet man. Treats me real nice and dear." Mattie Mae gave me a stern look.

"Don't fret Sugar, "said Miss Ann. "She only want him cause he gone get that 'surance money when his daddy die. Way I hear that ought be any day now."

"I don't loves him for his money. I loves him cause he good to me," Mattie Mae got awfully haughty 'bout thangs, that is 'til Miss Chayonne cut her short.

"You sho loves quickly. Who you gone loves tomorrow? Minute ago, you making mud with them tears, cause somebody put a hole in Ray. Now you loves Bugeye. You done had fire in yo drawers for a long time gal, you betta get hold o' yoself, for you be roun' here pregnant and hiding."

Mattie Mae just sat on down. Everybody sat real quiet for a few minutes. You could almost hear the winds on the gnats and the mosquitos flapping as they flew by. Course it was feeling to me like them 'squitos was doing more feeding than flying. After Miss Chayonne got tired of me swatting, she made Earl James build a fire.

"Hey! Miss Chayonne you got snuff on me! Damn!" Ray Charles, not the singer, but the boy with the funny shaped head; he lives next door to Miss Chayonne. He likes to ride his bike in front of her house.

"Watch yo' damn mouth boy! I don' told yo' big head ugly ass not to be riding close to my spit spot. Now you better get on back over there, 'fore I fix it so you won't be able to ride that there bike. And take this wit' you."

I couldn't believe she spit on that boy on purpose. Earl James, Cliff, Miss Ann laughed like fools.

"He ain't gone come back over for a couple of days. When he do, it'll be after that prim and proper mammy of his come over here and call he'self tellin' me off. Last time, she come over here, I sat here and listen, real polite like." You shoulda seen Miss Chayonne demonstrating for us. "Then I tells her, that sho is a fine pretty dress you got on, nice shade o' yellow, I would sho hate for you to get snuff on it while you visitin', so maybe you oughtta take yo' l'il nice, nasty a . . . , I mean behind home now."

Mattie Mae was falling out, "What she do then Miss Chay-onne?"

"I tell you what she did, I was hyere that night," Earl James jumped up. "She went flying off this hyere porch and said 'untamed woman, save her Lord'. Chayonne say 'you bes' hope the One True Lord save you.' I ain't never seen hips that big, move that fast."

"Oh oh." I tapped Miss Chayonne on the knee. I saw my daddy's car pulling up the street and could see from a short distance through the front glass, mama looked mad. I told Miss

Chayonne I probably wouldn't see her for a couple of days. After all, I did lie to leave the house and had come to one of the three places I wasn't allowed. The other two was the Do Drop In and the pool room, course they ain't as much fun and informative as Miss Chayonne's porch. At least not to me. And when Jamie come up here, that's Miss Chayonne's niece who live in the house on the path behind her, then I really have a good time. It ain't like I drink hooch wit' 'em. Miss Chayonne don't 'low it. But mama and daddy don't listen, they just have a fit.

"Sugar," said Miss Chayonne, "I sho hate to talk 'bout yo' mama, but she jes as saddity as this woman over here."

"Yes, ma'am I know, sometimes she gets on my nerves too."

"Well, you be respectful and go on home. Look here," she pulled me close to her. "If yo' daddy start to give you a hard time ask him, how come he jes don't bring you by here when he comes."

Boy, I laughed about that all the way home and was waiting for just the right time to use that line. That one and the one that I wasn't supposed to know. That mama and daddy got married cause she had gotten pregnant for the third time and that I got two brothers in Savannah living with my auntie. Miss Chayonne was extra drunk that night.

Now I gotta sit home for two weeks. Cain't go nowhere but school and church unless I'm wit' mama and daddy. But that's all right; cause I know sure as gnats gone come to Georgia in the summer time, Miss Chayonne gone be on her porch telling tales.

My Skirt Wasn't What He Wanted To Be Beneath

"Y̲ou lying son of a . . . You really didn't think I would figure it out did you. Got me giving everybody all kinds of explanations and . . . you lying son of a . . ." I closed the brown wood framed door to my office so hard, it knocked the certificate just to the left from its hook. The temperature in the room rose just as quickly as my body heat. While this was probably an argument more appropriate for a non-professional environment, it was too late to curtail it.

"What is your problem? I have no idea what you are talking about!" He didn't even allow his demeanor to show any degree of concern.

Why do people look you in your face and lie; even when it's obvious they've been busted? Busted! That's what this is - a clear case, of I caught your faggot - smiling in my face - not even realizing your stories aren't connecting - prancing - obviously attracted to a man's man behind in a lie. I forcibly pushed past him, and placed myself in a power position on the edge of the desk. This was my moment and I refused to allow him to deflate it.

"This is what I am talking about. From the moment, you laid eyes on that photo of he and I you were flustered. Like a hooker caught in action."

"My God, I can't believe what's coming out of your mouth. I am not listening to this. And I am so mad at you for confronting me like this." He simply scratched his head. Was that a sign of ensuing defeat?

"Oh, so mad at me. You're looking to dip into my honey, but you're mad at me for confronting you. Tell you what, I'm going to sit here quietly in my office and take a moment to pray my temper doesn't get the best of me. But at the same time, I'm going to pray that it does. And since I'm hoping for temper and not temperance, I'm going to come out of my jewelry now." I leaped from the desk, pulling the diamond hoops from my ears, and removing the watch just as quickly

"Look, I only did what you told me to do - and you wanna be mad. That's why you don't have a man."

There was something very relaxing and yet chilling about my four-inch heels landing in the meaty portion of his groin. There was something very calming yet masochistic about the sight of my mahogany wood frame crumbling with the glass as I smashed it over his head. It was just, well, smashing. And yes, I did say him. Ain't that some foolishness? I'm nearly 40 years old; I can smell a married brother ten miles out, but can't smell a sucker right up under my nose.

Honestly. I think I had smelled him. The aroma of some things was just so prevalent. But, I look at life like this, I got a whole warehouse full of shit I don't want anybody to know about; hell, I graduated from a closet before I hit 21. So, with all of that in my house, I figure you always give people the benefit of the doubt.

After this last episode though, I think I'll just go with giving them the doubt. What is that saying? If it walks like a duck, quacks like a duck - then it's a duck. But that's not necessarily true, I mean my duck didn't walk or quack like a duck, at least not a duck dipping in another pond. Or did he?

I met Shorty at a marketing convention. It was a brief encounter, yet I was struck with his - I don't know - with his ability to be fine. He was almost the spitting image of actor Avery Brooks, in his days as Hawk on the television show "Spenser For Hire". That was a black man that didn't get enough camera time for me. But this guy, Shorty, was every bit of him. With a classic baritone speaking voice that made every part of my femininity dance. We introduced our selves and parted shortly thereafter. A few weeks later, a chance meeting about the purchase of land for an entertainment complex brought us together again.

In the five years I've known him, I can't honestly say we have a relationship. We do. We don't. We do when I start to wander off. We don't when he gets too close to me. We do when he slips up and spends half the night in my arms. We don't when he walks out from yet another half night not having touched me in a sexual sense. We do when something in him says this is the woman, this is her. We don't when something in him says this is the woman, this is her. The cleaning lady eyed the photo of he and I on my desk one night. Laughed and then started crying.

"Miss Ruth, are we that funny looking together?"

"Naw sugar bear." (That's what Miss Ruth called me her Sugar Bear - because no matter what time of day or night, she found me at my desk, I would be eating that stupid cereal with the bear on the box.) "I'm laughing because you can sure tell there's something between you two. He doesn't come around here that much anymore."

"No, actually I haven't seen him in a few weeks. That's what happens. We're close for a while, he's calling every day, and he comes by here and by house. We hold each other, watch TV and then he disappears on me. But I think I'm tired of that now."

"How long he been like that?"

"The whole five years I've known him. Miss Ruth, I know you're a Christian woman and you don't believe in fornicating and stuff like that . . . "

"But . . . "

"But in five years, shouldn't this man have tried something? I mean even if I said no, shouldn't he have tried something - touch it - touch the tatas - something?"

"Baby, you can touch the tatas hugging, that don't count. He got some stuff he need to sweep from around his door."

"Miss Ruth, what does that mean?"

"Can't say specifically with him . . . but look at his eyes Sugar Bear; he's in pain about something. You say you love him dearly - so it ain't like he ain't got no love - but he ain't got no peace in his flesh. Something's hanging around his front door though like that nasty old dog that keep coming to your yard knocking over the garbage."

"So, what do I do Miss Ruth?"

"Do you love him?"

"I don't know anymore. I really don't know."

"You know, you don't wanna think about it. And that's because you got an idea about what's around his front door. The truth hurts, but sooner or later, you are going to have to face it."

Miss Ruth was right. I did have an idea about what was lurking around his front door. It all happened so strangely. Or maybe it didn't. Had I have listened to Jerome two years prior, I could have stopped it then and my heart wouldn't be laying sideways, asking what in the hell are you doing to me now. Jerome and I have been good friends for a good seven or so years. He is adventurous, fun loving and always trying to get me off to some exotic destination and of course, I never have time. My girl Sheila says the whole world will go on vacation and I'll still be behind my desk. What an exaggeration!

Jerome, Shorty and I ended up at the same restaurant one night. I was talking to a group of friends; Shorty was heading to the restroom and Jerome was just coming in. I remember the encounter so well because I heard Jerome clearly and with definite recognition speak to Shorty, and Shorty responded, cautiously but with definite recognition. I wouldn't have given it a second thought, except for two things: Jerome's prefer- ences in men, and the fact that Shorty lied to me when I asked if they had met previously. Jerome was much more candid about his knowledge of Shorty and he knew that what he had told me devastated me. Yet, he said, "girl, if you love him, love him, just know the truth - at the end of the day, one's penis has no conscious."

And then there was Wayne. Wayne came to work for Where Marketing as an intern. A clear mama's boy, prim, proper, hiding his ghetto fabulousness - let no one know you're ghetto. The buzz in the office was the buzz, you know he is - no I'd say. Ask Jerome he'll tell you - no I'd say. You know he is Gloria - no I'd say - he's not, he's a mama's boy.

"Your brother is a mama's boy Gloria," Sheila was growing tired of my denial. "Still he getting as much female nooky as the all the guys in the office combined. That ain't mama's boy, that's gay."

I can't believe she said it out loud. Now, I am going to have to face that obvious truth. Especially considering the stirring in my gut when he first noticed that photo of warmth and companionship that sat on my desk. Two things said something is wrong with this scenario. One Wayne recognized a man that only looked this way in the last three years, but said he hadn't seen him in about seven years. Two, he said,"I need to give him a call and see how he's doing." Then, asked if his number was still the same; but proceeded to call out a number he's only had for six months. He just lied. Here's how the lie went.

Wayne said that he had met Shorty, Mr. Cleary, some years prior when he took a summer job at the beginning of high school at his parents' former company. He said Mr. Cleary had left to take a position with a company in Atlanta so that he could be closer to his daughter. That reason for leaving was also contradictory to the one Shorty had given me - he left because he felt he wasn't effective anymore. In any event, Wayne went on to say that Mr. Cleary befriended him and would often teach him little things. I let it ride. Even though his little busted car now held, what, four lies.

That night, I asked Shorty about Wayne. "Yeah, I know him; I hadn't seen that kid in years, man, since I left his father's company. I ran into him about a month or so ago at a networking thing. He's working for you now?" His face did a strange thing, a movement that he hid by pulling the wine glass close to his face.

"He's interning." I placed a tray of cheese and fruit on the coffee table next to the recliner. I made note of the uninvited presence of tension as we talked.

"Why the curiosity?"

"He seemed a little thrown off by our picture sitting on my desk."

"I didn't know you had one there. Why?"

"Because the last time you came over here, which was what, two months ago - you didn't see any around here and that lead to a 15-minute argument."

"That's here, but at work, you know I'm a very private person." The turn of his back from me and the conversation nailed the head on the proverbial coffin.

"So, no one at work should know we're seeing each other."

"We're friends. I don't have a wife, a girlfriend, I'm not dating. We're friends."

I heard my subconscious remind me that I had just purchased that crystal tray and shattering it against his head would be wasted money. "You're full of shit, get out. How can you stand there and tell me that? What kind of fool do you think I am? Is what Jerome told me about you true?"

"Where the hell did that come from? I told you not to ever mention that punk's name to me."

"At least that 'punk' is honest with me; I don't know what the one standing in front of me is."

"What the f . . . I'm leaving." He nearly knocked my Zinfandel from the counter, trying to make a quick exit. His skeletons were falling out.

"You did it again. You really did it again."

"Did what?"

"You got pissed because I asked, you got enraged because I mentioned Jerome, but you didn't deny it. You have never denied it. It's not even that that's killing me. It's the fact that you keep lying and the more you do, the more I know."

"You keep listening to that punk. How can I have a relationship with you and I can't trust you not to believe what people tell you about me?"

"How can I have a relationship with you and I can't trust you to know that when I've told you I love you unconditionally I meant that - but which you am I loving? Oh. But, hell. Doesn't matter. Because, you don't have a wife, or girlfriend, and you're not dating anyone, we're just friends. Disappear, man. Dis-a-damn-pear!"

And then there was Wayne again. Two days after that argument, I called Shorty and made one statement, make up your mind - it's me and a relationship or I pray you have everything you want in life without me. Stupid move. Guess, I just wanted to feel like he was giving me some kind of thought. It's been two months and I haven't heard from him. I finally hid the photo in my desk. I figured in another month, I'd throw it away all together. Then one cloudy, boring afternoon, my curiosity got the best of me. Not about Shorty, but about what Wayne's connection to Shorty was or is. About what Wayne wants from Shorty. So, I set a scenario.

"Wayne, have you talked to Mr. Cleary lately?" I dipped the cinnamon biscotti into my cup of chai tea, debating what I hoped his response would be.

"No, not for awhile, why?"

"Well, I gave him an ultimatum and he took the one that didn't include me."

"Oh really." Said with much more interest than I wanted to hear, but he didn't look up so the twitch to his face may not have been a smile.

"Do something for me." That twitch I hoped was not a smile, nearly burst from his face. He was having a hard time controlling his excitement. I was growing weary.

"What would that be?"

"Call and see how's he doing for me . . . ."

I didn't have the chance to finish giving the directions before Wayne jumped up and retrieved the phone in a quarter second. While I thought, again, to finish the directions; I couldn't because he had dialed the number. As I walked out of the room I could overhear his disappointment when he was advised Mr. Cleary wasn't in the office. Later that afternoon, Sheila would have to tell me that my asking Wayne to call was not a good decision; because it was obvious Wayne's desire to speak with him was clearly that - desire. And now when I confront this heifer, he tells me he doesn't know what I'm talking about. And Shorty, out of nowhere calls - like everything is everything. Two months, not a call, not a visit; but the same line of bull, "I care about you more than you know. I think about you constantly." But you don't call until this heifer calls you from my office.

Shorty-Malcolm Cleary met Jerome and Wayne in the same types of settings; a gay bar and a private party. Jerome and Wayne met under similar circumstances, and you should have seen Wayne's concern when Jerome burst into my office one day to tell me we were going to Jamaica for the weekend whether I wanted to or not. I sure do need Jamaica now. To get rid of the thought that I may no longer be attractive enough, woman enough, loving enough, dependent enough to attract a man that only wants a woman. I'm going to Jamaica with Jerome this weekend because Shorty really had not rejected opportunities of passion with me because he was concerned about where that would take our friendship; but he'd rejected me because he was more attuned to being pleasured by a male touch. I was going to go to Jamaica to cry on the pearl beaches and sip rum and fruit juices until the pain went away. Because for the first time since high school I felt like the cool guy had gotten over on the fat girl and I had been played by two punks in a pod.

The morning before we headed off to the sun-warmed waters of Ocho Rios; I stopped by the office to entertain a meeting with Wayne. He had been very tense since the day that frame accidentally broke over his head. As I flipped through the pages of Gloria Mallette's new book, ignoring the hell out of Wayne's rambling words – I smiled. There was, after all, something very gratifying about not accepting Wayne's letter of resignation and telling him he had to be mature enough to work with me, despite his invasion of my personal space. I tore up the picture of Shorty, never wanting to feel his arms around my waist again, and let the pieces fall slowly but definitively onto Wayne's lap. I laughed and closed the door behind me leaving him sitting in the dark.

A Daughter's Secret

"Thou shalt not uncover the nakedness of a woman and her daughter, neither shalt thou take her son's daughter of her daughter's daughter, to uncover her nakedness; they are her near kinswomen: it is wickedness."
   Leviticus 18:17

D
ark blue funk would hang like smog in the room. Its burdensome assignment often choking life out of situations that were already maddening and grim. Weariness had become a constant companion. Weariness and anxiety. I could feel it, far too often in recent years, pressing on my heart.

She fumbled with the three-dimensional puzzle for nearly an hour before she uttered her first word. I understood that. I knew that staying quiet, in her uninvited indoctrination into the sorority of assaulted daughters, was normal. You did it, even if you didn't want to. I was invited to participate in her kind of shenanigans when I was about 12.

My brother, Zay and I, were two blocks away from home playing with some kids from school. He knew everyone in the neighborhood that surrounded our home. If he wanted to go play, ride his bike, ride his skateboard, or anything else that involved him leaving the house before our parents got home – he had to take me. We were at Corey's house. The boys were going through comic books in his room. Corey's sister, Jace, asked if I wanted some chips.

We went into the kitchen to get them and were headed back to the bedroom when her dad, who I knew, told her to take the garbage out and feed the dog. "Wait right here for me," she said. Right here, was in the living room, near the chair where Mr. Jake sat watching TV. He asked me to hand him the TV Guide from the table. I didn't give it a second thought. He and my dad loaded trucks on the dock together. He had been to our house to play cards and for parties.

I handed him the TV Guide and he commanded my hand. He grabbed it, his old, rough, ashy hand squeezing mine. My hand turned red from his pressure. He stroked my hand with his finger, telling me how pretty I was and how nice I had filled out. He asked if I had a boyfriend. He asked if I ever let a boy touch me. He asked if I thought he and Corey were cute. He pulled me closer to him, almost right in front of him. He asked what I had beneath my shirt, and he tugged on it. I told him nothing and jumped. He squeezed my hand again, holding me in place. He stroked my thigh with his fingers. I was in trouble. As his fingers crept up my thigh, his hand moved towards the inside of it. That hand was rough and dry. I heard the boys and Jace outside, they had gone out the patio door; clearly, they forgot about me.

He said, "don't be scared. Come sit here on my lap." He pulled the hand he commanded, pulling me ever closer toward him. It was my brother's urgent voice that broke his intention. "Melissa, come on! I just saw daddy's car turn the corner." A second later he was at the door, and that dusty old hand released mine. I ran home crying, never telling Zay or anyone else what happened. He never took me over there again, especially since the next time Mr. Jake came over to play cards with dad and his friends, I sat in my closet – shaking. In fact, Zay would never leave me alone with any boy – or man – after that.

I watched Peppa Broullaint with the puzzle. Her box plaits wound up in a bun. Although her records, and she told me she is 14, her demeanor and her face are younger. Her maturity, intellectually and emotionally, would fluctuate based on the conversation. I worked with many shattered vases like Peppa, hoping I could help them pull those pieces together into breathtaking and whole re-creations.

Peppa, had a light about her, that fought with the dark blue funk and I liked that. Something about this little fireball in the help-a-sista-out tshirt and cut off jean shorts made my notions to give up counseling sexual assault victims seem moot. I scribbled nothing noteworthy in the black portfolio notepad, on my new glass top desk waiting for her to break the ice. When she did, I knew that we were going to get somewhere, finally. It took her three sessions. One of those three, she cried for two hours, her face nestled in my armpits. I would stroke her hair, rub her back, breathe deep so that she would match my breaths. That day, she needed to feel a maternal reassurance.

"Do you know how it feels to be dirty? I do. I use to tell myself, I have to scrape away this dirt."She pulled the burgundy pillow with the gold, copper and yellow flowers, from the couch onto her lap, brushing her hand across its surface. Her eyes glazed over, as though that pillow knew more than she would ever say.

"What does being dirty mean for you? And tell me, why do you use the word scrape instead of wipe or rinse?"

"Because . . . feeling dirty is when you touch your own skin and it makes you sick. And it's like you see somebody that you know is nasty and you know they're going to touch you with their nasty. You feel like if you don't get to the bathroom quick, you're going to go on yourself. Then you're more dirty. Or dirtier. Or whatever. It's dirty."

"And you said scrape . . . " I know she didn't want me to see the tears, because her left hand became a quick and awkward extension of the side of her face.

"Because the dirt, was too too thick. It was thick, thicker than mud and it would stick to me. So, I thought, you know, maybe that old steel brush is still under the bathroom sink."

"That sounds dangerous, Peppa." Her gaze caught mine. Resolution sprang from her youthful brown eyes.

"I knew it could tear my skin off. I didn't care." She regressed before me. Laying the pillow down softly, as if she had to be careful not to harm it. She began to tug on her hair and her shirt. "I just didn't want to be dirty anymore. I was going to use the steel brush and a little bleach to scrub off the nastiness. That's how we clean the dirt off the barbecue grill. Do you barbecue?"

"Well, I don't do a lot of barbecuing. I do love a good barbecue rib or barbecue chicken sandwich though. Can you barbecue pretty well?"

"I guess we won't be doing it a lot anymore either. Mama, taught me how to do the sausage on the grill. She said he could teach me to . . . Well, nobody wants barbecued dirt."

I repositioned myself next to her, and inhaled deeply. She followed suit, allowing the breath to remind her that she was in a safe space.

"I was so scared. And I was so ashamed. No matter how hard I scrubbed, the shame stayed. It never stopped. Never. Not even now. You think I'm pretty?"

"I think you are as cute as a baby doll; and that hairstyle is fly on you. Do you think you're pretty? When you look in a mirror do you see your beauty?

"I don't. I know I'm not pretty. I can't be pretty cause pretty don't attract ugly. He always told me that though . . . 'you are one pretty girl. Got to make sure boys don't take advantage of you.'"

I breathed deep and held the breath, 1 – 2 – 3- 4; and repeated the action. She continued to follow my lead.

"I felt like a landfill. I feel like a landfill, big old garbage thing, that's me. I tried to make myself ugly, so he wouldn't think I was pretty. But mama would fuss because she said I was looking like a raggedy throw away. It didn't stop him though. And I would cry, hoping he would stop, but . . . I kept crying, real hard, like water coming from a sponge when you grip it real hard. But he wouldn't stop. Not one time did he stop."

She needed to know her cries of STOP were valid. She needed to know that her voice yelling, STOP, had power. We played a combined version of old school childhood games, Mother, May I and 123 Red Light. But in this game, Peppa was in control, if I touched her in any way that made her uncomfortable, she would yell STOP and immediately I backed off. If she screamed STOP and I didn't back off, she screamed it again with a counter action to my action. We would have to do this exercise several times until she knew she was worth the value of no, and the respect of stop. I took note of the easier breaths, and the shift in her confidence.

"You know what I wonder? I wonder if my momma cried too. If his dirt, his hard, nasty dirt fell on her too."

"There is a difference in his actions with you and how your mother and father touch . . . " I misstepped. Clicking the switch on the table lamp, nearly knocking my cup of coffee over, I thought about how to redirect her, or pull as much of the controlled anger out of her as possible.

"Don't you dare call him my father! HE IS NOT MY FATHER! Oh God, how I wish my real daddy was here now. "I'll always take care of you Peppa." That's what he said. Always take care of me. That's what a father does. That's what he was supposed to do."

Her tiny shoulders descended into her chest. In just that movement, her power took flight - again. I asked if she wanted to stop for the day. Her little face rose. Tear-soaked eyes and cheeks begged to be held.

"I hated my father for awhile. If he hadn't died, then nothing would have ever happened. Me and Cassa would still be with our mother, mama wouldn't be mad at me. I wouldn't be talking to you. I'm sorry that was rude. You're nice and all but . . . "

"It's okay. I know that talking about such personal violations, even to someone as nice and all as me, is not easy. Tell me about your father."

"He was tall. He had these weird long fingers. We had a basketball hoop in the front yard, and my mom says as soon as I could stand up without wobbling, he had me shooting hoops. It's been about five years since he died. I was nine. He got a cold, went to the hospital and never came home. Mama started messing with him about a year later. We never liked him." The memories of her father pushed her from the couch. She focused instead on the photos and certificates hanging in different parts of the room. She would straighten frames that were not crooked. She would read a diploma and look back at me.

"You went to all these schools? You like your father? He's your real father?"

"Yes, he is my real father and he is a good man. I love him dearly."

"I hate him! I truly do." She realized the volume of her words. "I'm so sorry, I don't mean your daddy. I mean my mama's husband."

Peppa explained that she had a whole vocabulary of words that she used to describe – as she called him, this time – her mama's husband. Curious about the other words, I pulled my large Post-It note pads from the closet and stuck several sheets on the whiteboard hanging on the peach wall. From the second drawer of the file cabinet, I grabbed the art kit. Draw him. Draw arrows pointed at him, labeled with the things you call him. Get it all out, I said, so that you can recognize the things in men – and people – that can potentially bring you pain. Her version of his face on the canvas must have sent a rod of fear through her. I could sense her spirit taking flight. I stood against her back, sending my strength to her.

"At first, I didn't think anything was wrong. I mean he would touch me. He'd pinch my booty. One time he kissed me, put his tongue in my mouth. I've never kissed a boy, you know that? Is that how you do it? I mean with your tongue like that?"

As I watched her drawing move away from my directives, and into the visuals that still haunted her, I deflected her last question.

"I think that is a conversation we will need to spend a whole session on. Keep going." I smiled. She sort of smiled. I would take that as a sign of hope.

"After awhile, I started praying all he would do was touch me. I felt like God was busy with someone else, somebody was going through something worse. So, I kept praying and I knew sooner or later, God would hear me. Then I started praying he wasn't touching Cassa too. Can I tell you something? Every time, when it was over, he'd talk to me like nothing happened. That's strange huh?"

"What did you want him to say Peppa? Is there something you believed he should say to you?" I remembered Mr. Jake, and I could answer the question for her. I wanted him to say, now you know I'm wrong and I shouldn't be touching you. I'm sorry. But this, wasn't my moment; it was hers.

"I don't know. I just thought so. Sometimes he would slap me, tell me not to fight him next time. Sometimes he would say stuff like, "didn't your mother tell you to clean up this room this morning." Like nothing happened. So many times, I wanted to cuss him out. But I knew I couldn't say anything. Would you have cussed him out?"

"I think everyone does what they believe will keep them safe, in a dangerous situation."

"Would you have runaway? I thought about that too. But Cassa would've been by herself. But I really wanted to cuss him out loud enough for the whole street to hear. But I knew I couldn't say anything. I would just think about picking up my things. All my dolls. I should throw them away now, huh?"

"Why would you throw away your dolls? Didn't you tell me your dad always bought you dolls?"

"Because dolls are for little girls, I don't feel like a little girl anymore. I was going to save them for my daughters. Now I don't want them. The dolls and the daughters either. Please don't ask me about that. I don't know why I feel like that. I just do. I can protect them, if I don't have them." She turned and looked me deliberately in the eye. Then asked did I understand she would protect her unborn daughters from her pain. I didn't push the envelope. "People do a lot of crying in your office, huh? That's why you keep all these tissues? You cry sometimes when people leave here?"

"I do cry. I cry because I feel horrible that you all were forced to go through some things that no child should ever have to. I cry because sometimes I don't know if I can help you heal. I cry because I hope you all understand that beyond the counseling, I want you to learn to love your pure self – purely."

"You think he loved me? I don't think he loved me or Cassa or my mama."

She had become her sister's keeper. The definition of that encompassing the literal protection of that baby's virginity, her power, her strength and her value. How could she defend her sister, when she had no one teaching her how to defend her own?

"One day she came to me and told me he was strange. She said she couldn't go swimming no more because of him. I didn't understand that. Cassa can swim better than most of the kids at the Y and she's only nine. That's when I figured he must be touching her, I got real . . . like nervous, but . . . yeah angry at the same time. I started breathing real hard.Cassa (she tried to find her way into her breathing exercises, in and out) why can't you swim (in and out) anymore? (In and out) Cassa stop crying (fill and empty). Why Cass (fill and empty) can't you go swimming (in and out) because of him? She didn't say anything, she started hitting me. "It's all your fault Peppa, why don't you like it when he touches you. It's all your fault." Why would he do that? I let him do what he wanted, and he told Cassa I wouldn't, so he could touch her."

I rose from the desk and proceeded to walk towards her. She held out her hand, signaling me to stop. I respected her decision. She stood from the couch and walked over to the bookshelf, thumbing through the candy in the antique Wonder Woman lunch box.

"I took her swimming at the Y. That way he couldn't look at her. She doesn't even have real titties yet. How could he do that?" Her fingers grasped the sides of the bookcase. "She said he put her on top of the washing machine and played with her breasts. Cassa's only like this big." She released the shelves and faced me as she measured her sister's height with her imaginary ruler. "I . . . how could he?"

I extended the tissue box to her, when she pulled her sleeve to her nose.

"Do you have daughters?"

"No. I have 3 boys, all under 12." I pointed to their photos on the top shelf of the bookcase. She retrieved one and smiled, courteously, at their images.

"Is it different? You know doing that with someone you like?"

"Doing – that – Peppa, is something you should do only with someone you truly love. That's why your introduction to it, has created so much damage and pain and confusion."

I wasn't sure she fully understood the meaning of the words. She didn't, however, descend into her sadness.

"Okay, love? You don't feel dirty?"

"No, but we will make sure we discuss that in the session when we discuss kissing. I need you to understand Peppa that there are things that happen in the definitions and design of relationships that you still aren't aware of. I am hoping that I can help you begin to see the lighter and more awesome side of that. Listen, can you tell me how your mom found out about what was happening?

"My mother found out because Cassa and I told her. She got mad at me. She told me to stop telling such lies and to stop making Cassa lie with me. Before I knew it, she jumped on me, Cassa jumped on her and we were fighting each other. I still don't understand that. Why was she mad at me? I didn't give it to him. I swear I didn't. I didn't want to do it, I never liked it. I swear I didn't. She kept saying you're lying Peppa, say it. I couldn't say that. Then I would've been lying. She was so mad. Cassa was on the floor crying. I felt strange, like I didn't even care anymore."

I pulled her back to the couch and held her. Her body tense and tight.

"I told her I wasn't lying, over and over and over. She didn't hear me. "I don't want to hear this young lady. How can you be so hateful? I didn't raise you to tell lies." I just started screaming. HE RAPED ME MAMA. HE RAPED ME. HE GONE RAPE CASSA TOO. YOU HEAR ME, HE'S GONNA RAPE HER TOO. She slapped me, again. Later that night, I heard her in my room. I was sleeping with Cassa. I peeked out the door. She was packing my clothes. He raped me. Why was she packing my clothes? I never gave it to him. I promise you I didn't."

"I know that you did not give yourself to him. You need to know and I need you to say it out loud for me – that he had no right to touch you, to violate you or to have sex with you." I held her face up, but her eyes would not rise to the occasion. She didn't really believe that truth yet, and I had to accept that – for the moment.

"The next morning, she didn't say anything to me. She didn't even say anything to Cassa. He wasn't there. Then the next day, I took Cassa to the Y. But she got really scared in the water and almost drowned. Some boy bumped into her by accident, but she thought he was trying to touch her and she was trying to get away from him. We almost didn't go home. We were just going to walk around. We could of went to our aunt's house, but then we would have had to tell her our secret. I think that's why my mama didn't send me off. She would've had to say something."

When I asked what finally happened that got her to me. Her eyes grew wide. She seemed shocked at the question, which shocked me. It was not a difficult question, not based on the things I'd queried her about before – even when she didn't answer.

"I left Cassa sitting on the porch, while I went across the street to see Ms. Randolph's new baby. Cassa is scared of their dog. She didn't want to go. I wasn't there long, I promise you. We heard her screaming. I shouldn't have left her, huh? We went running across the street." I found myself fighting to control my breaths, this is the part of too many of these stories that enrage me. After all of these years, I still can't help the righteous indignation that shoots through me. "Her panties were around her ankles . . . and her legs were open and she was shaking . . . and he jumped when he saw Ms. Randolph . . . and his pants were unzipped . . . and she started throwing stuff at him. When he ran, we grabbed Cassa and ran across the street. She called the police. But he left before they came."

In all that she had been through, and shared with the police that day, she still feared that her mother would hate her. Mom apparently told the police that her daughters have overactive imaginations, even knowing what her neighbor witnessed. Peppa struggled with understanding how and why her mom didn't believe them, when she raised them not to lie, and lying was not something either of them had been prone to doing. I offered explanations that I believed a wounded and disenfranchised

14-year-old girl could understand. In the offerings, I realized what she really wanted to know is why didn't her mother love her enough to trust her word. Why didn't she trust that her baby girl needed her to send the pain away, not fight her to keep it home?

"Cassa and I are going to stay with our aunt. I know I'm never going back to her. I feel different about things now. Ms. Randolph told me to stay strong. She says sooner or later my mama will believe us. My aunt says the same thing. You think she'll believe us? You believe me? God believes me. He knows the truth."

Three hours down, and Peppa grew quiet. That was fine with me; I'd gotten two almost smiles and she got a glimpse of the fact that she still held a wealth of power within. She stood in the open doorway, waved at her aunt down the hall and then turned to face me. Her arms embraced me, quickly and her head hung for just a moment. "Do you really think I'm pretty?"

"Peppa Broullaint, I think you are exquisitely beautiful, and no one will ever take that from you, because it comes from your amazingly attractive spirit and your heart."

I closed the door and listened as her footsteps grew distant, and cried; then breathed. The dark blue funk lingered in the corners of the room; but the presence of hope let the air of possibility move victoriously throughout - anyhow.

Tales From The
Gray-Haired One

It's such a mystic kind of vision. The way a full moon casts a glowing white shadow over the night. This glow has seen so much I'm sure. I believe that it has shined on heritages, earths, waters, lives wasting like thieves in the night. I suppose most people would be intrigued by the darkness. But not me. I am drawn to the white shadow. For there in that glow, is what truly gives the darkness its meaning.

Papa is a dark man. A brown so deep is his skin, but it is simply just your basic black in disguise. He wears a glowing crown of white and silver bush upon his nearly six-foot frame. A bush that not only reflects the lineage of some majestic tribe in Africa, but of a cavalry-worn tribe native to America. Though to hear him speak of it, his whole heritage began and centers around an old wooden house in the closeness of a small country town. Through the locks of his crown I see so much.

Slicked back with water and pomade. His younger days, or should I say nights spent juking, drinking and telling lies in juke joints. Picked out in a curly 'fro. Looking presentable enough to find a job in the big city. Brushed back so the curls lay out as waves flowing towards his neck. He really wants to be left alone to enjoy whatever when he wants to. Yes, the variation of his locks reflect what life has taken him through.

Night falls around us. Each mouth has a story to tell. Kick back time doesn't come too often. No. Not often enough. We're kicking back tonight though, me, Whipple and surprisingly even Brother-dear; and Papa seems to like that. It is an especially dark night for some reason. That's probably why someone up above cut the lights on in the form of a full moon. I surmise that it is on these especially dark, full mooned nights that more babies are conceived. Of course, the only time that conception might be more plentiful is on a rainy night. That's the real reason Brooke Benton treasures those rainy nights in Georgia.

We watch the darkness. As I look towards the moon, I quietly thank the Gods for turning on that moon; because it has given Papa a will to tell his gray-haired tales. So, I pop the top on a can of soda, pull a pillow close to my breast and watch and listen to the darkness. It is the simple offer of a drink that forces the memories into the conversation. "No thanks," said I. "I don't drink. I'll stick to my Pepsi."

"Oh yeah," laughed Papa as he slapped Brother-dear on the knee. "You might not drink now. But, there was one time when you was home sick from kindergarten with the measles. I pours me a drink and sat it there on the table while I went to the bathroom. Come back and the drink gon.' Now, I know I poured the drink. Ha' mercy. My baby done drunk that whole glass. Thought, ole big red was gon' get sick. Hhm, shoot. It just brought them measles on out. Didn't even bother her either. She just sat there playing with that little ugly doll that had more hair than she did."

For the life of me, I can't figure out why I'm so embarrassed. After all, many years and experiences have come and gone since then. The light from the moon now seems to fall like a spotlight on Papa. My daddy, the leading man. As I watch him scratch his locks, rub his round and full belly, and stomp his feet in laughter; I imagine what a child he must have been. Papa and I share a quiet nature. Like me, I know that silent front hides many secrets and unexplained emotions.

"Papa. Now why you wanna pick on me. Don't let me tell them what Daddy-man told me 'bout you when you were playing baseball." I give him this stern, watch your mouth look now. Papa doesn't flinch.

"Huh, I coulda played for the nigra baseball league!"

I quickly placed the soda on the table. Rising to place my hands on far too plentiful hips.

"Now Papa. That's not what I heard. What I heard is while you did a pretty good job of hitting the ball, you had a problem when it came to running."

I plant myself on the floor at Papa's feet and pat them. These are the feet that had to walk 20 miles to and from school, every-day, until they walked him to his first job at 13.

Whipple chimed in, challenging Papa's version of the tall tale. "Daddy-man said Papa couldn't make it to first base with-out tripping over his own feet."

"But see . . . see . . . I was so l'il 'til my pants would slide down and get caught up 'around my ankles. That's why I'd fall."

"Yeah. Right Papa." I rolled my eyes at his hilarious observation.

"Well, wait a minute you guys." Brother-dear rose from the wood dining room chair, with the wobbly leg and stood facing the living room holding court. He looked like he was going to deliver some profound message. "I don't think Papa is the only one around here that had a problem running. I think you may need to refresh the memory of one of your sons." Laughter did not find Whipple this time.

"Well now, you know I'm 'gon do that. Ole Whipple . . . here it is a Saturday morning and your auntie whining, course she was always whining. TC you better go to that football game with your baby, make sure don't nobody hurt him. And if he gets hit too hard, then take him out of that game, cause ain't nobody gone be breaking that child's bones. God bless the dead . . . the woman was crazy, y'all old enough to know that now. Lawd, have mercy. She loved y'all like her own though. Yes, she did. Bless her crazy self."

"Your mind wondering old man, stick with the story." Whip-ple, tapped his shoulder, directing his head to Papa's nearly empty cup. Papa declined the refreshing of his drink.

E. Claudette Freeman

"Oh yeah. Saturday morning. I takes the day off from work. I don' told everybody in the yard, I'm going to see my youngest boy play football. Get out there in that hot sun, cracked two eggs on the sidewalk next to me, cause that's how hot it was out there. See what I mean?"

We all laugh at the way he relays his fables like they are certain gospel.

Whipple challenges him, "You pulling the truth man, aren't you?"

The notion that someone saw through one his tales, encouraged Papa to add his own dramatic flair to the "funning" of Whipple. "Hell no! And if you weren't so busy runnin' the wrong way, you'd a known how hot it was out there. Anyhow, old Whipple gets the ball, on the 15-yard line; 15 yards y'all that's all the boy had to go. I'll be son-of-a-gun, if for some reason that boy didn't lose his mind and turn around at the 15-yard line and run the other way. Here me and William is running right long with him on the sideline; yelling turn 'round boy, turn 'round. That doggone boy got to the 10-yard line on the other side of the field 'fore he turned around. Course by that time, William had don' run out there and turned him around."

"All of that and I STILL got the touchdown!" Whipple popped his collar, assured that he would have the last word.

"Well I suppose so; everybody on the other team was on the ground cracking up. Boy ran the wrong way." Check.

And then, came checkmate. "I kept my pants up though Papa, what you got to say 'bout that?"

While Papa and Whipple were battling with versions of something that happened close to 20 years ago; that other brother of mine – for some unbeknownst reason – was jabbing me like the brat he always was. By the time, Whipple and Papa were done sparring, I was chasing Brother-dear around the dining room table. Papa's hardy hand clap – one hard time – was our signal to cut it out.

I pushed him one last time. "Look at you, still running from girls. My name might as well be Sandra, aah!"

He cringed at the memory of the neighborhood chubby, tomboy, who was one real rough customer. "Don't even bring up that matter. That was not a girl. That was a monster!"

"She was sho'll crazy 'bout Perry. Kinda remind me of how I used to be after yo' mama."

Whipple positioned himself behind one of the dining room chairs, mimicking that poor girl. "Papa, she used to come stand at the gate, hollering his name. PERRY! PERRY! I know you hear me Perry."

"That doggone boy would run out his own house hiding from that girl."

"Papa, Whipple – listen. That's the only woman I've ever known that scared me. She was like what – six inches taller than me – and a good 195 pounds when we were in junior high school."

Papa bent over in his old recliner, sorely in need of new fabric and probably a new leg. We watched him curiously, not knowing which one of us he was coming for now.

"Sandra come to the house that time in her Sunday dress, hair all combed and she plopped right down on the stoop, she says, 'Sir, I'm gonna sit here and wait for Perry to come from basketball practice. If you don't mind.' I says to her, Sandra has it occurred to you that maybe Perry don't like big girls. The girl jumps up and says, 'Perry will so like me, or I'm going to beat that son of yours into the dirt.' I see Brother-dear coming around the corner, that boy looked up on the porch, saw Sandra and took off running. The girl took off after him like the dogs at the track . . . HERE COMES SPEEDY!"

"Homegirl took down three feet of fence to get to PERRY! And Brother-dear, knocked me down and ran right over me trying to get away. Papa, me, Amp, Po-boy, Daryl, we took off running behind them. When she caught him at the corner, she had him face down in the grass, sitting on his back, trying to kiss him. It took all of us and Mr. Harold to pull her off him."

"Wondered whatever happened to her." Brother-dear shook his body, as if the memory was something he didn't want around him.

I enlightened him with what I knew. "Sandra, got married about seven years ago, to an overseas basketball player. Seems all that chasing of you, helped her lose a whole lot of weight, and she was turning heads."

That news tickled Papa who then provoked the boys into playing cards with him. I decided to keep my money in hand. Papa tends to create rules as he goes no matter what he's playing, tunk, Georgia skin, 21 . . . doesn't matter. That's just him. I think he gets a thrill out of believing he can still pull the wool over our eyes. Hand, after hand, the trash talking ensued.

"Daddy-man ever tell you all 'bout that time he almost shot me?"

"Yes, he did." Whipple played a card, and from the look on Brother-dear's face, it was not what he was hoping for. "But you tell the story. Let me see if you tell it like him."

"If I 'members right, I musta been 'bout 14 or 15. I was 'posed to be home after working at Mr. Campbell's 'bout 9 o'clock. Now, Mr. Campbell had don' tol' me to go straight home, cause I was already out late, and mama'd be worried. And then too, you know in them there days, colored folks couldn't be out too late, lessen they was looking for trouble.

Anyhow, I runs into ole' James Earl and Sonny Lee, got ta dranking that buck. Sonny had done took it from 'neath his mama cupboard. Next thang we know Deputy Clark telling us it's 11 o'clock. He said, 'get on home 'fore ya mammies be crying cause you in jail.' I get out to the house; and call myself-gonna sneak in through the window. 'Fore I could find some-thing to climb on, that crazy dog o' daddy's got after me. Next thang I know Daddy standing at the door wit' the shotgun."

"I bet you it's that same shotgun, he tried to teach Broth-er-dear to shoot, and when he pulled the trigger, it knocked him clean under the dining room table, ain't it Papa?" I asked, pinching the oldest boy in the bunch on his neck.

"Same one, I believe that's the only one he knew how to use. Anyway, I sees daddy standing there with that gun and I got up that pecan tree so fast. But see Daddy didn't have his glasses on, so he couldn't see it was me. And then again, I ain't wanna tell him, cause I knew I'd get a whooping.' I be doggone if daddy didn't start shooting up in the tree. I started to just hollering MAMA . . . MAMA . . . .MAMA. Mama come running to the door, hollering "Oh Lord, don't you shoot my baby fool, don't you shoot my baby, put that gun down 'fo' you kill you own chile."

It seemed to warm me. For the first time in my life I noticed that Papa had the same expressions Daddy-man had when he told me the story. I remember that pecan tree, that failed as Papa's hideaway. We played around it often as kids. It was beneath that same tree, that Papa's cousin Jimmie Ray, used to make a fool of himself pretending to me a master of Kung Fu.

"Did you get a whooping still Papa?" Brother-dear queried, already aware of the answer.

"Did I? I ain't ate a pecan since. That's how bad a whooping I got."

Papa leans back on the couch, resting his hands atop his silver and white crown."No sir. Ain't ate a pecan since."

"Now wait a minute Papa, that is not why you told me you don't eat pecans, let's check these stories you be telling . . . "

Whipple played a card on top of Papa's, checking both the tale and the move he'd just made.

We were kicking back that night. Blessed that Papa could remember all the memories and fables of his youth and ours too. But kicking back is something we don't do so much now. No; not too much at all.

Big Girl's
Brother

The way he was moving . . . weave and bob . . . zig and zag . . . eyes had to be on fire with the moistness of his sweat. His face was washed in anxiety and sweat, anticipation and sweat, the taste of victory, the fear of defeat must have been pounding in his heart. And he sweated. Breaths plunging through his puffed cheeks as he ran. Running and zagging, it was like they didn't even see him. His arm, on the left, straining from the weight that he held. His arm, on the right, throbbing as he thrust it, maneuvering it like a standard shift to balance himself. Push away from walls, snatch gates from their hinges . . . wipe the sweat that never stopped coming.

Man, he was running. I bet he didn't even hear the noise behind him, or next to him. He was out running all of that. I couldn't believe it. His style like an Olympian. Yeah, yeah, like Jesse Owens. Was that Jesse's spirit I saw routing him on? It seemed like he ran for days, though, it was actually probably less than an hour. But man, was he running. And, finally, he did outrun them all. He sat for several minutes behind the heavy bushes that edged the walls of the old Montgomery house. It sat back from the street, so there was no way they would have spotted him. He calmed his breathing. He checked the gift he was to present. He rose, content that it was okay and headed to make her smile.

"Gregory, a TV, I can't believe you bought me a TV. And a color one at that. Wait 'til the kids see. Thank you, Gregory. Thank you." She hugged him, her eyebrows and forehead wrinkling with that a hint of knowing, and a wave of refusing to believe. He smiled from ear to ear, glad to see her smile again – about him anyway, after causing her so many sleepless nights for so many years.

"Aah, it ain't nothing Big Girl. My big sister deserves a brand-new TV. Whatever I can afford. Just my way saying of sorry. Cool?"

When Karen smiled, it seemed to make everyone else uneasy. As pleasant and pretty as she was, she rarely smiled anymore, not even with the children. Gregory couldn't understand that. It bothered him. Karen has always told him to smile. A smile let's people know you're warm inside. Watching her smile, Gregory wondered if his sister's warmth was leaving and if his stupid ways were the reason for her cooling.

They fiddled with the knobs on the TV adjusting everything just so. Getting the greens to match Karen's curtains, and the reds to "match my big, perky home grown tomatoes." She loved it. But not too much, cause knowing Gregory -- it -- like him wouldn't be around too long. Together the two, big sister, little brother, sat on the yellow plastic floral-covered couch admiring how much younger Dick Clark looked in color. They were laughing, sipping on iced tea with the grounds fighting with the ice cubes at the bottom of the glass. They were at home one more time. And not even the slamming of the door disturbed them. The voice of Karen's husband boomed against the walls.

"What the hell is that? And did you bring it here?" Charles knocked Gregory's feet from the coffee table, standing before him, his pride dangling, beaten from his sleeve. Gregory's eyes sought patience from his sister's face. Karen's eyes sought patience from Charles. "Don't look at me like that woman. You know very well; I didn't put this here TV here. And you know very well that if this here nigga put it here, it's hotter than the devil on a summer day."

Charles was right and she knew it. But she didn't want to. Gregory was tired of being accused of stuff he did do. But to allow Charles to demean him was not part of his program.

"I can't bring my sister a birthday present without you thinking I stole something." Gregory leaned forward on the sofa clasping his hands between his knees. Karen leaped up. The expectation of the building argument pounding in her head.

"Now Charles don't start. It's a nice TV and it's a gift. Gregory has a job now."

"Doing what? And is it legal?"

"Why you just can't give him a chance?"

"I'm tired of you tossing and turning night after night, worrying 'bout this tired nigga . . . "

Gregory stood between them, his young back just inches away from his sister's worried face. She spoke around him, slowly rubbing his back.

"It come in a box Charles. Styrofoam pads and all."

"You know what Big Girl," Gregory's eyes did not blink. He stared defiantly past Charles' broad shoulders. "It ain't no need for you to worry. I'll take it on outta here. I ain't gonna cause . . . "

The boys suddenly tumbled into the door so hard, the coffee table flipped over. Cigarette ashes falling all over the place, making the photo frames that hit the ground too, dusty.

"Uncle Terry here. Uncle Terry here. Everybody talking ma . . . ."

"Yeah ma. It's all over the place. Damn! Look AJ, this got to be it."

Karen scolded Ronnie about his cursing. Still she knew the excitement of a new color TV in the house had overcome him. Looking into her tired face, Charles posed the question she hoped he'd overlook.

"What everybody talking about AJ?" AJ didn't hear the question. His attention was commanded by the brief visitor to their home. It was a command broken by his father's heavy hand against the back of his head. "I said what you talking about?"

He tried to rub the sting of the hand away as he spoke. "The whole neighborhood talking 'bout how Uncle Gregory out run the police."

Karen quickly, supposedly unnoticed moved to the TV, pushing the knob to the off position, and snatched the plug from the socket. Gregory stood his ground.

"They must be talking 'bout somebody else. I got the thing from Sears and Roebuck."

"You sho'll did Uncle Gregory. That's what Uncle Terry said. Chase started at Sears and Roebuck."

Charles threw his long, charcoal arms in the air. His hands falling together in the pounding fashion of a preacher trying to drive his point home.

"Number one. Terry Ernest ain't your uncle. He's a bail bondsman, bounty hunter, whatever. And while he 'bout much as kin, he ain't your uncle. Number two, Karen if he here, that means that TV still belongs to Sears and Roebuck."

"Big Girl I'm leaving. I ain't gon' cause no problems in your house. And no matter what I say, somebody just will not believe I actually could have paid for the thing. I'm sorry I even bought you the thing." Gregory pulled on his sneakers. "I'll call you tomorrow Big Girl. Boys mind your mama."

He walked off towards the kitchen awfully fast; almost like he was trying to catch a fast-moving train. From the whispers near the TV, he was dashing, hoping he could and would ditch Terry. Gregory's face seemed to be computing the amount of time he had to get out. Terry is a systematic kind of person. He saw the boys down the street, talked to them, and gave them each a dollar. He stopped at Miss Margarette's candy house to get his self a hot sausage and a pack of Now-and-Later candy- cherry flavored - for his daughter. He would bite the hot sausage and turn around to get a fifty cents soda. Gregory hadn't cleared the kitchen entrance way before the arguing ensued.

"You drove my brother out again."

"Woman, the boy bought you a stolen TV."

"The TV was in the box. It was in the box Charles. AJ stop changing the channel like that."

"Box or no box Karen. It's stolen."

"Aah daddy. It's nice. 'Sides Uncle Greg had to out run 10 police cars . . . "

"It was 12." Terry walked through the kitchen, Gregory standing beside him, a solemn look on his face. "Still can't figure out how he outran all them police cars, with a big old color TV under his arms. Boy, got some skills, I guess."

Big Girl hugged her brother tight. Her tears landing where sweat had dripped hours earlier. Terry seemed almost sad, "They may not give him a bail this time. You know he violated probation."

Charles threw himself on the couch in a sitting position. Tapping the boys on their shoulder, pointing them to their room. The look on his face, his body warning them not to protest.

"Don't cry Big Girl, I said I'll call you tomorrow."

"Karen, you put your car up last time, I don't know . . . this time . . . "

Charles foot landed hard on the table. "Won't be nothing this time. My damn children have seen you so much over the years they think you family. Hell, they call your name in prayer now. He sitting this time Karen. I mean that Terry. He sitting." He rose slowly, deliberately. As he pulled the spare set of Karen's keys from his ring, he approached Terry. "Here, take the car. Have your boy out there drive it off."

"Come on Charles, we know each other, let's work something out." Charles' laugh made them all jump.

"Terry. He going to jail. You taking that car. I'm watching my TV tonight. Karen gonna cry herself to sleep again and this nigga here will have us all back in this same situation soon as he gets a chance."

Karen dusted knick-knacks, wiped ashes from the covered couch, burned the rice for dinner and left her wifely duties unfulfilled that night. Gregory called the next day. No bail.

Probably two to five. Don't cry Big Girl. Karen would of course cry, the next day and several other days.

"It's gonna be okay Gregory. I'll tell the boys. We'll drive to see you, no matter how far. No, Terry didn't take it. He said the store manager said he heard you dropped it while you were running and he didn't want no broken merchandise. Charles said we could keep it for all the trouble you caused. No, I don't watch it too much; but Charles says the same thing you did, Dick Clark looks so much younger in color."

My Mama's Blues

The blood poured from her arm. She glanced down at the needle. I could see it in her eyes –concern. Yet there was no sense of urgency coming from the nurse, so I didn't panic. When she looked up to see if I had noticed what was happening I smiled reassuringly and she seemed to relax. Not wanting to alarm, I walked over to the nurse and very politely told her that there better be a damn good reason she's got blood pouring from my mother's arm to the floor; or I would assure blood poured just as freely from her.

The urgency in her motions increased. The urgency of the pouring blood decreased. My mom seemed to feel better about the situation. I sat in the white-walled, medical instrument decorated surgical prep area as my mama prepared to do battle with cancer again. I couldn't remember if it was the third, or fourth time in the last few years. This time I looked at her as she lay there waiting to be wheeled in to surgery. I was terrified. The beeping of monitors, and heavy suctioning sounds of breathing machines did nothing to pacify the fear.

Why did I have to see her blood pour like that? Why did it seem like the whole room was moving in slow motion as the nurse wiped the blood from the floor? Where would I be if my mother's blood didn't drip through my veins? It is really so defining, how watching a very productive vein eject the blood it normally houses, makes you question the mortality of people you never imagine being without. Or for that matter, how it makes you question your own mortality.

A fighter. That is my mother. And therefore, I am a survivor. What does one have to do with the other? When you are raised by a fighter, you have no choice but to recognize the fight, get in it and survive. At least that's how I see it. Mama motioned me to the bed where her arm was now perfectly bandaged.

"What did you say to that nurse? You weren't rude, were you?"

"Now mama . . . you know me."

"Uh huh, that's how I know you cussed that woman. You got the numbers for the people I told you to call?"

"Mama you know I hate doing that. I have to be so nice to people . . . "

'You don't have to call who you don't want to. But do call your brother and do call Lacie. She'll be real concerned. And make sure them idiots put my papers through at work."

"Yes ma'am. Anything else you're going to worry about as you head into major surgery? Or should I just take over worrying about a bunch of insignificant stuff now?"

"You always been a smart aleck. I love you. Get something to eat and take your medicine."

"MA! It's called 33!"

"DAUGHTER! It's called I know. I'm the one who gave birth to you."

What do you do with a mother who is twice as stubborn as you are and growing more so every day? For a long time, I was convinced that my mama didn't like me and I that I have some ways she doesn't like either. But it is okay with me now. Because whether she accepts me has nothing to do with if she loves me. That's what I figure. If I'm wrong . . . Oh well, life goes on and I am clinically well-adjusteddespite it all. Still, there is something about her latest bout with cancer that has me concerned. I know mama is not going to die. I prayed about this whole surgery and my spirit is light, so she will come through again. This is just a new fight for her and when you've been in the ring as many times as she has, you're smart enough to beat the competition before your foot even touches the ground.

I picked up the phone and dialed the first name on the list. This is really one of those phone calls I hate making. It will, I assured myself, be a short. One ring. No answer. Two rings. No answer. Third ring. I prepared to disconnect.

"Hello. Somebody there?"

"Hello Auntie Pearl. Mama wanted me to call you and let you know she's having surgery today."

"Surgery for what?"

"A mass they found near her breast. Just making sure it's not cancerous and can be removed with no problem."

"Cancer. Hhm."

"Hhm. What does that mean Auntie Pearl? You have a question or something?"

"Naw, it's just a shame your mama has to go through that there."

'It's cancer Auntie Pearl. Cancer. And yes, it's a shame. But praise God, she's made it through every step with flying colors. It sure is shame you can't come be with her."

"Well, tell her I'm praying for her, and call me when it's over."

"Uh-huh. Sure, Auntie Pearl. I'll do just that."

For some reason my aunt has convinced herself that my mom is suffering from cancer because "she a smoker." Mom has not smoked for almost 20 years. I love it. Fear begets ignorance and ignorance begets . . . well whatever it begets, it ain't good.

"Hello, Mr. Moore speaking."

"Hey baby brother. What's with this Mr. Moore stuff? I changed your diapers boy."

"You know you ought to stop telling people that. It kind of blows your game when your sister tells people she changed your diaper. How's ma?"

"They just took her into surgery." I knew I would start crying. There never is any pretense with my brother and me. I can be the strongest thing, until he gives me that what's wrong tone. Then, I'm just a big mushy crying mess.

"Come on now baby girl. She just went into surgery. You know ma has pulled out of tougher bouts than this. What's really bothering you?"

"I was in the pre-op room with her. And the nurse hit a really active vein so blood was gushing all over the place . . . "

"And you imagined mama dead?"

"Not so much that. It was more about all the petty arguments she and I seem to keep having. I'm like a black sheep."

"Girl please. This is OUR mama we're talking about. We both are black sheep. Mama is hard sometimes, that's just her way. I don't pay any attention to it. Besides we've been around mama how long?"

"All our lives."

"Right. Right. So, we both know what she's going to say before she even says it. Like when she thought Angela and I were seeing each other again. How did that conversation go?"

It eased the moment hearing us both recite one of mama's favorite opening lines. "Now baby, I ain't trying to get into your business. I think you just ought to think about what you're doing."

I chuckled. "I know you're right baby brother. I guess sometimes I just wished she would leave some things alone, you know."

"See I think you have it harder cause you're a woman. She can't tell me my dress makes me look too fat. Or that my haircut makes me look too old. Or I should probably wear this color with that color. But I guess with mothers and daughters it's different. Y'all supposed to be reflections of each other, aren't you?"

"I guess so. But don't you reach an age where your mama should stop trying to play dress up with you?"

"And how would I know that? Mama hasn't dressed me since I was what 11, 12? I'm going to tell you again what I always tell you – mama will have her moments; you have to live for you and do what you want to do. But I do have to admit when it comes to our mama – doing that is a lot easier when you live out of state."

"Oh, now the truth comes out. You left me here with her for your peace of mind."

"A man's, got to do, what a man's got to do. Mama is going to be fine you know that. And you know she's gonna wreck your nerves because I'm not there. And you know she's gonna find something wrong in what you brought her from home or whatever. Just don't let it work you. "

"I hear you. And I know you're right, but not letting it work me, is easier said than done. I'll call you tonight. Love ya."

"I know you do. And stop standing in the white man hospital letting him see you cry. Be the strong sister that you are."

"And just think I thought we'd have a whole conversation without me having to bear arms."

"And the struggle continues baby sister. Love ya."

I have had this conversation in one form or another with Jarrod since we were in our mid-teens. We could never figure out which one of us was really the accident. That certainly seems a cold way of thinking. I really don't believe mama was harder on us than any other mother was on her children. It just seems to me that at a certain point in an adult's life, you need to wait to offer your opinion. But no, that is not the case with my mama. And it bothers me to no end. Jarrod is right . . . it is different for mothers and daughters. Because my mother's acceptance of me is ultimately very important, and the older I get the more comfortable I'm able to pretend it isn't.

During a conversation with a writing teacher one day, I made the comment that if I wore a strapless dress to a business dinner, my mother would disown me and then kill me. Her question in the form of a reply to the statement stumped me and haunts me to this day. "What does it mean when grown women say their mothers would disown them? When do you become a woman in your own right?"

I don't know what the whole disowning ritual means or entails. I do know it is a probable possibility with my mother. My fancy, my style, my creativity (that's what I call it) has often been her embarrassment and therefore I've often been made to feel guilty about it. When did I decide, I didn't want to be my mother and why is that such a horrible thing?

Six hours later the procedure was over. Everything was removed – the mass, the lymph nodes – no other signs of trouble. Mama was taken to her room and I could go up when I was ready. Though I knew she would be fine, the burden of her exposure to cancer again, lifted from me. Mama has been very intelligent about her bouts with cancer. She's asked questions, gotten various opinions and she's done her research. And whatever she has learned she's made sure Jarrod and I learned as well. That has made this even easier.

As the elevator ascended to the tenth floor, I remembered the argument my mom and I had about my decision to write for FACES magazine rather than take the job with the Miami Herald. For me it was an easy choice, yes, the Herald meant more exposure, but working with a black publication was important to me. I wanted to be a part of the movement that was relaying our stories accurately, from our own perspective. Mama thought I was being too black for my own good. I chose my path though and went in that direction. Every time I fell on hard times, mama was quick to point out that I would have no paycheck problems if I had gone to work for the Herald. Bottom line, I finally told her, accept my decision or don't talk to me about it. I didn't get a phone call about anything for a good two weeks.

Already conscious, mama was reaching for the telephone when I entered the room.

"And you would be trying to call whom?"

Her voice was barely audible through her labored breathing. "You. You weren't here when I woke up. I thought you went home."

"I wouldn't have gone home mama you know that. I was downstairs in the family waiting room; that's where the doctor just found me."

"Did you call everybody?"

"Everybody mama. Jarrod sends his love and in his own way he's praying for you."

"Did he say he was coming? I guess I ain't important enough though."

"Ma, please. Jarrod just started his job a month ago. He's been waiting for that position, don't make him feel guilty. You know he loves you and if he could be here he would."

"So, he's not going' to see me until he gets a vacation?"

"I didn't say that mama and neither did he. How about we call him later tonight?"

"I would think he'd pick up the phone to call me."

Ding, round one and the winner by a knockout is Essie Moore. Still the undefeated crazy argument champion of the world. I knew that battle was coming and yet I still didn't see the first punch. How did she put me up against the ropes and beat me down before I even got in the ring? Round one was for Jarrod. That meant the next bout was for me. Realizing that the attack could come from any direction, I did the smart thing and retreated to the bathroom. It was an anal process. I checked my breath, my teeth, combed my hair, put on lipstick (which I normally don't wear), assured my earrings matched my outfit. I made sure my shirt hung right, and my jeans didn't look too tight. They were by no means tight, but the appearance of the same could be a jab point. I went down my checklist. Yes, I had made all the required calls, I cleared her voicemail, and I made sure her leave paperwork was processed at work. I was clear. I quickly wiped down my temporary porcelain boardroom and stepped out to face my contender.

"I thought you fell in in there. You constipated? Maybe if you ate some real food sometimes and not all that fast food you wouldn't be constipated."

"I'm not mama. I was . . . "

"Have you been taking your medicine like you're supposed to? Probably don't do any good anyway. I don't like that doctor of yours. I keep telling you to call my doctor."

"Ma, you don't even know my doctor. He is very good. I'm healthy and he watches out for my condition. Look ma, let's not argue. I called everyone on the list and everything is taken care of per your instructions. You need anything else?"

"I told you not to call the people that were gonna aggravate you."

"Nobody aggravated me, ma. Everything is fine."

"Your tone's a li'l sharp. If you tired, you need to go lay down. I keep telling you, you don't get enough rest."

"I work for myself and an independent publication ma, sometimes you have to burn both ends of the candle to make ends meet. I'm fine."

"You wouldn't need to burn both . . . ."

"Ma. You sound exhausted. Why don't you just relax and go on to sleep? I am going to go lay down for a little while and I'll be back this evening. Do you need anything from home?"

"No, I brought everything with me this morning."

"Okay. If you need me or anything have one of the nurses page me."

"You going over to what's his name house? I know he lives close to here."

"Probably. It's closer to here and your place. And his name is still Roderick ma. It's been Roderick for two years."

"Well I won't disturb you then. In case you busy. I'll just wait for you to come back."

I couldn't help but chuckle. Only my mama between hard to catch breaths, could, in her own special way, ask if I was going to have sex with my boyfriend. Only my mama. Where did the health argument come from? That wasn't even on my list. Look, right here . . . calls, pick up mail, stop newspaper, take pills to keep mama from tripping . . . oh damn, I was wrong, I must have over looked it.

Mama was right. As soon as I walked into the door, I securely placed myself in Roderick's arms and urged him to make love to me. Even though he protested saying maybe we should talk about it, instead of running from it, he did make love to me. Roderick laughs at my mother and me. Laughs at the way she interrogates him in very polite tones. If he asks I would certainly marry him, based solely on the fact that he can handle my mother. That is an admirable trait.

Do we really grow up to be our mothers? If we do, can we still be our own women in the interim or even more importantly in the end? The second round of intimate distraction would have to wait. Mama pages. Beep. Thank you for calling, please leave a numeric or voice message. Beep, enter your pass code. You have two messages. First message, 4:32pm: Tiffany this is your mother. I need my dark slippers, not these pink ones. Second message, 4:33 pm: Tiffany this is your mother. I want to know what time you're coming back; you've been gone almost two and a half hours. Oh. I guess you're busy.

Round three – mama remains the knockout champion. Now I know that battle wasn't on my list.

A Tree That Bares
No Fruit

For the Lord had closed up all the wombs of the house of Abimelech, because of Sarah, Abram's wife.
    Genesis 20:18

I felt like I was an unwilling character in a stage play. Funny, but this play I had written myself because it is, after all, my life playing itself out. Yet, it seemed for the past few years, I have been an outsider looking in. Not really understanding all the emotions and promises of life that were thrown at me and then snatched away. Chance wanted to be a father. Initially, I did not have the same passion or desire to be anybody's mother. My life had been such a traumatic drama. I feared my experiences would become my child's.

While, the intellectual side of me knew that I absolutely controlled my ability to create a loving environment for a child, and a family; I kept reliving my reality theatrics. I willed myself to stay in the moment. This was not the time to write another scene that would end in death. Yet, there was something very deadening about the pain. It stopped time, took away the importance of anything else. Took away the importance of the joy that was supposed to be fulfilling. Like a sharp and brutal knife, the pain cut through me. I could feel it slicing the things inside that made me a woman. I squatted just to give the pain somewhere to go. This pain felt like needle-point hands yanking at my tubes, ovaries, uterus, but nothing would come. I waited for the gush of blood that I felt building in me to pour out, but there was nothing.

I can't remember how many times, I've found myself holding on to this desk; it has given me comfort repeatedly, when the pain visited. "Okay God, whatever you want, just please make the pain stop. Come on Lord," I heard myself saying, "You know this speech already. Why is this happening to me? Why can't I just have a normal pregnancy and be over with it? Why can't I just have a child and clean up puked formula, like normal mothers? Just make the pain stop. Don't let this be the end."

Six forty-five. I was already half an hour late for dinner with Chance. There was no way he was going to know that I was doubled over behind the leather chair in my office, again, clinging to the oak leg stand, praying for an end. I had become familiar with my torment. So much so, that I've learned just how far I can push myself and still put forth the appearance of normality. You know I love my man more than anything. I couldn't let him see me like this again. I couldn't see that sorrow in his eyes, watch him choke back tears.

I clung to the carpeted walls of the office building, stopping when someone came near and searched through my purse, so that the grimace on my face had a purpose. I etched my way to the parking lot; pausing from time to time to regain my composure. As I pulled into the parking lot, I freshened my make-up and slid the comb through my hair. In the final moment of practiced deceit, I removed my contacts and put on my glasses. Certainly, I didn't want the fact that I had been crying to be so obvious.

"Hey handsome, haven't been waiting long have you?"

Even when Chance was pissed, he had a way of calmly disturbing the peace. "Fifty-five minutes late, you broke your own record tonight woman. Is everything alright?"

His arms momentarily erased the pain. I could have easily collapsed in his arms, safe in the knowledge that no matter what happened this time; he would be there for me.

"Everything's fine. Just got tied up behind that desk again. You know how I get."

"Yes, I do. But you're four and a half months into this pregnancy, and we agreed you were going to take it easy. Didn't we?"

"I don't want to fight, baby."

"We're not fighting. I'm reminding you that (1) we've already lost two children, (2) the doctor didn't want you working at all this time and neither did I and (3) we agreed that since you would not take a leave of absence, you also would not pull any extra hours. Was this not a conversation we had?"

"I didn't mean to snap, alright. I'm fine."

"Was this not a conversation we have previously had?"

"Yes, it is. I said I was sorry. I'm fine, really I am."

"Tarah. We have to be really be careful this time. I'm putting my foot down now. I want you off the job . . . now . . . I don't want any lip . . . I don't want any buts . . . . I want you off, now. "

"Chance . . . "

"No . . . Tarah . . . NOW! What happens to me if something happens to you"

"We are going to be alright baby. This time, everything is going to be great. And I've already put on ten pounds to prove it."

"Is it only ten?"

"Oh, see that is not even necessary. What happened to all that, woman you're glowing and all that, huh . . . ? Huh?"

I really do love Chance. He's stubborn. No. He's pig-headed and too damn direct. But he's a good man. Three months after we were married the pain started. For months, I lied, telling myself they were all in my mind. But there were too many times, when I found myself clinging to the toilet, my desk, the couch; too many times, I buried my face in the pillow to keep Chance from hearing me scream; too many times, he'd held me trying to control the trembles that would overtake me.

When I finally did go to the doctor I had driven myself crazy with thousands of possible problems. Cervical cancer, any other reproductive cancer, ectopic pregnancy, every possible disease and illness had possessed my body. At least in my mind. The diagnosis was uterine fibroid tumors.

We ordered dinner, and I felt one of the familiar grabs near my lady mechanism that indicated something was up. I kissed Chance on the cheek and told him to get more rolls, and headed to the ladies' room. I know that I entered a stall. I know that I felt those hands pulling everything connected to my ovaries and uterus.I felt the deadening pain, and I felt the warmth of my blood trickling down my legs. Although I was all too familiar with this feeling, and I knew blood pouring down my legs was not a good sign, I began lying to myself. No, I will not lose this child. No, this is not another miscarriage. Yes, I would be a mother this time. I saw a woman, and said something about husband, Chance and then I think I closed my eyes and laid down on the floor.

Everything else, was crazy. I was having a hard time determining what was real or what was one of the scenes I'd create – hoping the distraction would relieve the pain. That's what I hoped. I would pretend to be in a play or a movie and then this scene would be better.

SCENE - Hospital examining room. A medical worker is conducting various pre-labor procedures on a young woman, on me, as a young man (my God, even sweating and scared Chance is fine) stands by holding her hand and watching the action in the room with great anticipation. The young woman, me, while smiling, seems very distracted and bothered by the attention to the fetus being discussed around the room.

For a just a moment I turned my attention away from the monitor that everyone is watching intensely. Instead, I thought about the day I realized this child and I were lost searching for each other. There I sat in my artsy, warm color painted, very contemporary decorated home, massaging my pregnant belly - smiling. I felt it – I felt the product of a magical divinely ordained passion in my womb. I couldn't wait to hold the little hand and count the little toes. That feeling was fleeting each time though. And as quickly as it came this time, it left, still, for the most part I didn't understand the misconnection with this child in my womb. Or maybe, I did. Two babies had been denied, perhaps not connecting was a way of deflecting the loss to come.

But – the eerie misconnection took me back to the times in my life where I connected with nothing and no one and was always turned away. When I felt, my body tensing on the lonely hospital bed and saw some of the monitor levels began to shift, I tried not to focus on the pain that once again began tearing at my body. But the thoughts that did come ripped at my heart, at a time when it should have been filled with hope and prayer. I tightly closed my eyes and in between the desire to push, and the yells not to, I was becoming an unwilling character in another act.

SCENE and DIALOGUE: I was in an older home, very boxed in appearance. A younger version of me is arguing with a middle age woman. We are in a living room setting, while the place seems neat – there are some clothing items lying about the room, cleaning utensils have been pulled out- because I was always cleaning this trifling woman's house, like Cinderella. As the scene begins the woman, Miss High Mistress-Drunk Every Friday through Sunday-Get Foster Kids to get the Check-Madeline is surveying the room.

MADELINE – Tarah you better get in here and clean up this house. I told you I wanted this place clean when I got home. What you think, you stayed home from school for nothing.

TARAH (enters, speaking under her breath) No I stayed home to be your maid.

MADELINE – What'd you say? Your mouth the main reason you in a foster home. You better watch yourself little girl.

TARAH (begins crying in anger, tears grow in intensity) Why you even . . .

MADELINE – Why I even what? Let you live here. Where else you going? You 13, your brother 8, ain't nobody gonna take y'all. "Specially not him, he was a crack baby.

TARAH – How you know that? If we so in your way, then send us back. Send us back.

MADELINE – (steps towards her) Girl, you betta . . .

TARAH – Go ahead, please hit me. Hit me so we can get outta here. You had a party. I didn't. I wanna go to school. Johntay needs to go to school.

MADELINE – I got two others in this house besides you and your brother.

TARAH – And we all want to get the hell out. You don't love none of us. You don't care about none of us. You in it for the check. Johntay been wearing the same shoes since we been here, but I know you got a check.

MADELINE – Get out. Call your caseworker and get your fast behind outta my house. Tell her to pick you up on the corner.

TARAH – What did I ever do to you? When I first came here, you were talking about us getting our hair done together and going shopping and to plays. What happened? What happened?

The beeping monitors were driving me looney. They were adding stress to something I didn't want to be involved in. "Oh, God, Chance it hurts. I don't want to do this anymore. Please just let them take it. Let them take it."

I can't tell you I even know what he whispered in my ear. But whenever he thought it necessary to pull me close and whisper, I knew it meant I had taken him to an emotional level he wasn't comfortable dealing in. Excitement about the monitors and my screams continued. Chance's face was enthralled in so much emotion. I wondered if my face was the same to him. I wondered if it his heart was breaking, knowing it was becoming obvious, these demonic fibroid tumors were going to take this child too.

Chance wouldn't let go. No matter how I cried. How loud I screamed, he kept saying, "You and me girl – we'll do this together. Whatever happens, we'll get through it together." What was going to happen? As my body stopped reeling from the latest wave of pain, and a series of false labor pains that were wreaking havoc in my body, I focused on the opening shots of a documentary on foster kids that laid undone on my desk. Because it was so real for me, I struggled in completing the job and somehow now I was worried if my past wasn't going to allow me to walk into this new high in my future. I shook off the thought and went over the shots in my mind, trying to figure out if I was satisfied with the order of the stories. I could hear Chance begging me to stay with him. But with him, in that moment, meant feeling all of it. And, I couldn't do that. The scenes would cover the pain.

"I'm sorry baby, we have to decide this time. Tarah . . . Tarah . . . "

The activity in the room increased, and a chill and then a strange heat moved through me. The monitors, as I battled for consciousness, sounded like the song on the square the day I met Chance. The day I met Chance, the room was spinning now. The lights were yellow and then white, big and then little. The day I met Chance.

The crowd was thicker than the cafeteria mashed potatoes that afternoon. An impromptu step show was probably the only time you get this many Black students standing still in a court-yard. I turned to move past the steppers and disappear into the crowd on the other side of the courtyard, when he stepped in front of me. With one pound of his foot on the pavement, my whole self quivered and he awakened something that I never felt. With one pound of his foot on the pavement, he seemed to stop time and stop the yells from the crowd around us. And when he was sure he had my attention, his body moved into one smooth and majestic spin and he bowed at my feet. The crowd went wild and I ran to class.

After a full day of academia, I decided to exercise my creative poetic side and take the stage at ShyMike's. I felt like Nikki Giovanni was standing up in me. And Sonia stood in the wings of my spirit waiting to spew her lines of revolution and proper socialization. Ntozake had a different point of view that would dance from my tongue into the minds of the crowd. I stepped up on the stage. "My voice is deep," I said to the band, "percussion and a little bass guitar is all I need." They seemed to appreciate the challenge.

> So, I laid my head on a rock
> Someone said it was a pillow
> But what does a pillow really
> Signify,
> old folks fearing death
> would cry, don't take the pillow
> from beneath my head
> But move mine
> Cause I'm already dead
> I laid my head on a rock
> Avoiding the comfort of a pillow
> Cotton, down, duck feathers
> Whatever
> There was no comfort
> When you laid your head in one place
> Tonight, but
> Another place on another night

And yet another night
Another place
Pillow to pillow
post to post
A rolling stone
A rock is where I laid my head
What am I trying to say –
you are
Simply not listening
If the pillow
You offered me represented home
then I had no pillow
I had a rock
Cause wherever you rolled me,
Like Papa
That was my home
Never true – just
Temporary
Cause wherever you threw a rock
That is where I landed and
That is where my brother landed
And that is where my sister landed
And that is where
the baby your best friend will conceive tonight
But leave in the trash can
Will land
On a rock

A hush and sighs filled the room; the drummer shimmered on the snares to add dramatic effect. They had finally gotten hold of what I was saying. I scanned the room, pulled my hands into a praying fashion and laid them against my heart. Slowly, I let my eyes shift from one end of the room to the other and extended them in appreciation to the tables directly in front of me. My whole body began to shiver. I felt his foot pound on the pavement stopping my breathing for what seemed like eternity. I looked back and gave a nod and mouthed a thank you deeply to the band, unaware, until the drummer directed his stick towards the audience that I had gotten a standing ovation on my first night up. I stepped down from the stage and walked past him slowly, allowing him enough time to hand me a business card. Pushing the door open to the ladies' room I looked down at the card. Reading it with a laugh. Take a CHANCE! 555-9311. And just what chance was he inviting me to take?

I heard my husband's voice gently calling my name. "Tarah. T-bae. Can you hear me? Tarah, squeeze my finger if you hear me." I did what he asked, as best as I could. I released his finger and moved my hand to the emptiness near my belly. His hand covered mine. A drop of water touched it. The emptiness. His tears. It was over.

Months passed. They were difficult months. The doctor wanted Chance to allow him to perform a hysterectomy. He refused. Clearly, he understood the medical reasoning and concerns, yet, he thought that decision needed to be mine. He agreed that it was for the best, and encouraged me to consider it a viable choice. I couldn't bring myself to agree with that. No; I did not want to end up pregnant again. But, I did not want to give up my lady parts nor the opportunity to perhaps – finally – get it right.

All of it, added a level of strain and distance between us. This last stolen pregnancy, was on the verge of stealing Chance's desire to be a daddy, and my determination to make it happen. We argued about the surgery. We argued about adopting. We would even argue about whether the chicken should be fried or baked. I worked a lot. I created projects that did not need to be done. He worked a lot. He would come home and kiss me, if I responded, we'd make love. I guess that's what it was.

The distance would soon return with a vengeance, when Chance found out something I never bothered to share. His anger bounced off every wall in the foyer, the starting place of an argument I could have and probably should have cut off before it even started. At my request, he stopped by the doctor's office to pick up a referral. As luck, would have it, the doctor happened to see him.

"So, you'd been bleeding for a week or so before the night of the miscarriage and you didn't think that was something I should know?"

I froze. There was not a word or sentence coming to mind. "I . . . it . . . "

"Aah, so you still don't think there's anything to say to me? What the hell?"

He stomped towards the kitchen and all I could do was watch his steps. I tried to will the right words to my mouth. Nothing. "So . . . now that I think about it . . . that night at the restaurant, is that why you were late, were you in pain?" Nothing. "Aw, hell Tarah, really, really. Everything we've been through and everything you knew we were supposed to do . . . "

"Not we, dammit, ME. Everything I WAS SUPPOSED TO DO. ME, man, ME!"

"Seriously. It was all about you."

"You didn't feel that pain, Chance. You didn't feel that blood rushing from your damn body like somebody unplugged something in you. You didn't feel any of that. You don't get to be mad at me, because I didn't say anything. I didn't want to say anything else about fibroid tumors, pain, bleeding, miscarriages, what I couldn't do. So what, I didn't tell you I had been bleeding. There was nothing – nothing you could have done!"

Of all the things, I could have said, I'm sure that should not have been it. It was my truth, but it was not fair to someone who had cleaned vomit, cleaned up blood, held me while I was in pain; and someone who said he could find joy in being an uncle or godfather rather than see me experience another round of hell.When love stands in the midst of your pain, the way it has in our marriage, the last thing you should tell love, is go to hell, you're not as important as me in this. That distance turned into months – months turned into almost a year without a touch from my husband. Months of talking at each other, but never being engrossed in each other's ideas, ideals and words.

As I waited for him to come home, I thought about how we used to be. There are several things that I've always appreciated about Chance. One is the way this man looks good wet. I know that's not something that kindles the fire in most women - but it does with me. Chance has incredibly smooth skin, and naturally-rippled muscles that flow almost effortlessly from his chest to his abdomen to his arms right on down to his thighs and his calves. And when he is wet it is like watching ice cream melt beneath hot caramel, smooth and soft. Time after time, almost from our first time together, I'd sit quietly on the porcelain chaise in the bathroom and watch him shower. Watch him arouse me and leave me ready for his touch. Then I'd slip quietly out as he turned the knobs to the off position. I don't know if he's even aware of it.

I knew what my husband wanted. I knew what he deserved. When we met in college, I was still a scared, fractured young woman who was helping to raise a little brother, who was finally with a foster parent that loved him. Chance, became an amazing source of healing for both of us. I needed to honor that.

I would tell him that I made the call and set an appointment to begin the adoptive parent classes. And I would tell him after assuring that he knew I was sorry for my selfishness, and for forcing the intellectual and intimate passion that lived with us to leave. As he began his nightly version of Harold Melvin and the Blue Notes "Wake Up Everybody"; I set the candles ablaze around the room, poured the Mimosas into the champagne flutes and pulled the spreads back to the furthest end of the bed. Tonight, I would be ready for him. There would be no negative conversations. There would be no, what's up with you, nothing, you, same old. There would be no watching him slip into his t-shirt and shorts and go running, until his moment passed.

His vocals, broken and humorous, filled the bathroom and flowed out into the auditorium that doubled as our bedroom. Why did we have to get the full song tonight? I wanted to make love to my husband until he could do nothing else but fall asleep in my arms.

Finally, the song ended. The smile in his eyes as he entered our boudoir pleased me. His towel tucked about his waist, I handed him a flute, and asked if we would accompany me to a special set of classes to become adoptive parents. We danced in the middle of the floor for hours, knowing there was no music playing. There needed to be no more words; we needed to find our rhythm again, and I would dance in his arms all night, if that's what it took.

The phone rang for what seemed like forever before I heard Chance's voice inviting me to leave a message. I knew he wasn't at work, he'd only left home 10 minutes earlier. But I had to say what was on my mind. "Hey baby. It's me Tarah. I'm leaving you this message because I'm scared. I don't know if I can be the kind of parent I know you're going to be. I know how much being a father means to you and I promise you, no matter how long it takes, I'm committed to being the mother to the child your heart desires and deserves. I love you, boy, and I'm glad we're in this different kind of gestation mode. Just know, I'm scared; but I'm ready. And I'm rambling. Listen, you're the one chance I'd take over and over again."

By the end of the message I was in tears. The tears increased a few hours later when one phone call on that Wednesday evening, took away all the sting of the fibroids, the miscarriages, the nights of lost intimacy. Ahead of the tentative schedule they'd given us, the agency was ordered to make an immediate placement. The social worker remembered our story and was moved to act in our favor. It was about to happen.

Shortly after six, I felt myself growing very apprehensive. Chance was running late. I wanted to hold him for awhile before I broke the news. I needed to know that we were really, like for real, all right, again; and that he could allow me to mend the wound to his spirit this time.

"Tarah. I'm home. Where are you?"

"I'm in the kitchen. Your salad is on the table. I'll be out in a minute."

It hit me. I should do something so silly, but so special that it would make him laugh. While he tossed keys on the table and kicked shoes off in the corner of the living room, I ran like a kid hiding cookies to the bedroom. Quickly and quietly, I prepared to make the big reveal and open the door to this new family properly.

"Tarah? You all right baby? You need some help."

"NO. I'll be right there."

"I thought you were in the kitchen. Are you all right?"

"Yes, I'm fine. Get the salad dressing out the frig. I'll be right there, man."

As I approached the kitchen door, I peeked around the wall to see where Chance was. He had settled in the chair that faced the TV; I smiled. Perfect view for my surprise. I walked around the room turning up the lights slightly so that he could read my message clearly.

"Chance. Look."

As he looked up, I held one of the receiving blankets I never threw away, in front of me. Disbelief filled his face, he shook his head and began to laugh as he read the message out loud.

"Mommy said you have to stop and buy another blanket on the way to pick me up. I'm ready to come home. Are you coming now?" The man carried me out the front door, we were both barefoot. Fortunately, one of us came to our senses before we got to the corner, and we turned around to make ourselves presentable as sane adults picking up their new child.

I worked with a woman once that told me she and her husband had never been able to conceive. I still don't know how we ended up on that conversation. What I do remember is the message she got, from The Only Wise One, as she called God, that let her know it was still well with Him, and should be well with her. Some may conceive, some may carry, but you are called to love for those who couldn't.

Dancing In My
Own Mess

Rolling into consciousness from a night that left me feeling like I had had a full aerobics workout; I struggled to focus on the muted browns and beiges of the wallpaper. As they came into focus I realized that it was truly not attractive and I couldn't figure out why I chose it. Amid this blooming consciousness, here I lay humming that same stupid song as Diana's vocals banged in my head. "Good morning heartache, you old gloomy sight, good morning heartache, thought we said goodbye last night. I tossed and turned until it seemed you were gone, now here you are with the dawn."

What was this day going to hold for me? Let's see, would it be the cry-all-day-routine or the shop-all-day-routine? The frig is packed so maybe it will be the eat-all-day-routine. Then again, at this particular phase of my heart-battered existence it needed to be the get-this-shit-together-today routine. Here I am walking up on 35 like I'm in a freaking speed walking marathon, like a damn tornado through a toothpick factory, like a fire in a fireworks factory and I have yet to walk in one piece of knowledge. And that simply is, if you truly love you, then you won't accept dung from the thing that comes attached to the third leg. How about that?

Feeling the steaming hot water beating on my romantic bruises forced me to rewind my love video library. While it was certainly entertaining, it said nothing about who I am as a woman. It said nothing about who I am as a human being that deserves love without the games, the pretenses just to get and keep the sex and the heart stopping philosophies. Or, maybe it did. Since that it is more likely my truth, my tears fell as I scrubbed my medium-length natural kings and curls, slowing the video in my head to the scene that drove me to a state of duh and what the hell, last night.

Because the buzz from the liquid relief had not completely left my head I decided I wanted to share this pity party with someone else. Then I told myself no, maybe not, just get through this girl. You know what I think. I think every woman in you should dance no matter what the damn occasion. That's what I think about this whole love façade. I think you ought to dance when you lose your mind. Dance when you ain't got no tears left. Dance when that damn knight in shining armor is dancing all over your heart. And that's what I screamed into the phone when I heard the voice pick up on the other end, "EVERY WOMAN IN YOU SHOULD DANCE . . . "

"Ruth," I heard Charlotte's voice calling from the other end of the receiver, "baby you're drunk and you really need to give up that E and J philosophy."

"It ain't E and J Charlotte. It's J and B. I am a scotch girl, not a brandy one."

"Ah, forgive me for not remembering the name of your I-can't-keep-a-man poison of choice."

"Why Charlotte do I keep getting myself into these situations?"

Why in fact do I get myself into these situations? And why am I now, in that category of intelligent, okay drunk -at the moment - women who become purely stupid at the touch of masculine hands requesting my full hips – their juicy watermelon to be enjoyed on a summer day. And why in realizing that I've messed up again, am I wondering how long his scent will linger in my nostrils.

"Ruth, can I give you a piece of straight-up hard-core advice? Stop getting beat upside the head with a piece of man. It's time to understand that you cannot serve you on every plate."

"What does that mean Dr. Ruth?"

"Girl – here it is – ready, don't miss this now. Hold on. Here it comes. It's going to be so simple, the depth of it will mesmerize you."

"You're increasing the pain in my head."

"Here it is. Sex. Is sex. You get it as good as you throw it. It ain't all him. Every man that give you a piece, whether it's two minutes or all night, don't necessarily want more than the honey pot. And, oh, while we're at it. Sex, is not always an invitation or precursor to love or relationship. You're putting way more emotion into the action you're defining. Stop it."

Okay, I think I just got told. Charlotte knowing the gory and the glory details of every relationship I have ever had was accurate in her summation. At 34, I have been involved intimately, okay sexually, with about 12 guys. Whoo, that's a lot! Is that a lot? I feel like that's a lot. Quite honestly, I'm not proud of it, especially since I didn't get started until I was 20. Hell, now that I think about it, that means I basically screw somebody for a year and move on. I'm not proud of the fact that ninety-eight percent of those relationships have been with married men and the others have been with guys who were attached in every freaking sense of the word except legally. Yet, I poured my everything into those relationships and what grew was a bunch of stuff I can't even name and I never want to feel again.

"Charlotte . . . "

"I'm listening girl and stop crying."

"I know. When you spend holidays or birthdays with your man, what's that like?"

"Don't do that girl; it's not even worth it."

"Charlotte, believe it or not there are one or two things I've never told you. You know when shit makes you feel so low you can't even tell your girl- something's wrong."

"Come on boo. What would possibly make you that bad?"

"Last year, Christmas, we . . . I got all dressed up; kick ass red dress, cleavage showing. Little black drawers with the jingle bell in the appropriate place. By the time, Christmas rolled in and out, I was still sitting there waiting. I jingled my own bell . . . "

"Ru . . . "

"Wait girl, let me do this Charlotte."

"I wish you didn't have to."

"Me too."

I held the phone crying. Charlotte didn't hang up. Sometimes I really wished she weren't in North Carolina. I mean spilling your guts by phone can be therapeutic, but there is truly something to say about having a good friend standing in your face knocking your marbles back in place. At the cusp of losing my damn mind, I really wished Charlotte could knock some sense in to me.

"When I met Derrick, I was minding my own business. We kind of kept crossing paths at different social events. I liked his marble brown eyes and the way his big lips seemed to stay moist. But I diverted my attention whenever I would see him, because none of his signals were clear. Quite honestly, they never got any clearer. Common sense was never a strong point for me. That is, I guess, why I didn't heed the warning signals and leave well enough alone."

"Stop crying blue girl. Finish telling me what happened."

"I cooked dinner and arranged the candles on the dinner table. Girl, I put the holiday edition satin sheets on the bed. Charlotte the candles set the tablecloth on fire."

"Never showed huh?"

"Didn't even call until the third of January. She had family come to town unexpectedly."

"Uh, then he asked you to please understand. What happened to him saying he spends his time the way he wants to?"

That was it. He did spend time how he wanted to. Doing, hanging with, talking to, bugging, calling, loving, feeling, touching everybody – but me. Having half a man is better than no man at all. Didn't I hear that in a song? That is – for the record –

bullshit. What good is to your heart or your little black box to have half a man that you never see? Bills paid. Shopping easy. Sex often becomes an independent venture. And I don't have to tell me how to do it!

"Ruth, what are you looking for? All the trauma, all the games aside, what do you really want? And, add to your record, that half a man is never looking for a full woman. And, if he finds one, he's not going to try to help her overflow – he'll force her to subtract to feel better in himself. You get that?"

"I hear you. I do."

"So, what are you looking for?"

"I want somebody to love me a whole lot more than I could ever imagine loving his behind."

"And so, doing men who have no concept of commitment is going to get you that?"

"I don't . . . "

"Stop lying to yourself. If he's got somebody, where do you come in? I mean really where and how do you effectively come in as it relates to what you want in and out of your life. Damn Ruth, what do you deserve?"

"I don't know Charlotte. I don't know."

"Then close your damn legs and find out."

"Whew. That's really not a nice thing to say to your girl."

"Whew. And your crying and drinking is a nice state of life?"

I hung up on Charlotte, and sobered up from my after-passion pity fiesta.My problem this time was we talked about spending this whole romantic weekend together, jet skiing, driving up to the arts festival, cooking dinner together and it was never going to happen. The passion was magic. The cuddling was – aah, yeah. But. I ease out of bed and walk a few feet out the cabana doors to the bathroom, when I come out he was gone. Like a puff of damn smoke – gone. No note, no nothing.

And of course, he turned off his cell phone. I guess . . . my thing is . . . I don't even know what my thing is. I got what I let walk in and what I asked for.

I'm not a praying chick or a church girl, but still, I told God no more. No more attached brothers. No more married men. No more relationships where I'm the one that keeps getting knocked down on the list of priorities. No more not stepping away from the bedroom games long enough to figure out just what I deserve. You know I think I got lost in the game. I was playing so hard I never even realized when I started getting played. Honestly, if I was made to feel good and taken care of, it didn't even matter; until, not even feeling good felt good anymore.

Here's what kind of day it's going to be . . . I'm getting rid of that wall paper, throwing away every pair of sheets in my house, destroying everything that reminds me of any brother that ever stroked, kissed or tickled me; and I'm coming brand new. Bottom line, I believe my J and B philosophy, every woman in you should dance – so I'm about to straight get jiggy with it.

Sunday Drivin'

I was sure hoping Terry didn't want to drive today. She
always wants to drive; but we never go far enough when
she does. Anyway, it's my daddy's car and I should be able
to drive anytime I want to. But Terry's my best friend, so I share
equally with her all the time; except for my coconut candies.

"You can drive today Missy. I feel like just sightseeing."
That's what Terry told me. I almost didn't hear her good cause
she slammed the door so hard. When you slam the door, the
whole car shake, rattle and roll and the dust from the seat rise
up like a tornado tearing up the farm.

"That's fine Terry. Fassen your chair belt. I think we ought to
go to Texas today. How's that?"

"Well, I guess that's fine. Am I wearing the right outfit for
Texas? I should've packed an extra outfit. You know what them
pretty ladies downtown say . . . "

And we laugh really silly like and said it at the same time . . .

"A lady must always be properly dressed."

Terry found a piece of wood to knock on 'fore I did. That's
okay though, next time I'll get the good luck. Besides I was
driving and when you driving old Buttercup, you have to keep
both hands on the wheel. Old Buttercup will get 'way from an
in-ex-period . . . un-ex-pired . . . a person that can't drive too
good. You can't just let her wobble looking for no stupid piece
of wood. Terry know that. That's why she got the wood first, and
that's why she didn't want to drive; cause she wanted to get the
good luck.

"Terry, did you remember to put some water in our ther-
mos? Every time we travel you forget the water. We had to go
drive all the way to Paris, France yesterday wit' no water. Do
you have to pee?"

"No. Got better than water this time. I put some Kool-Aid in
it with some ice. That way when we finish the Kool-Aid, the ice

can melt into water. Then we can have two kinds of drinks on our trip. That's a good idea huh Missy?"

"We learn a little more every time we go away. What we got for lunch Terry?"

"I got half a hot sausage, a bag of potato chips . . . "

"You put the ketchup and hot sauce on them?"

"Yeah, yeah and I got two chicken wings out the 'frigerator. Daddy been nibbling on 'em all day, so mama won't even notice they gone. I figure we can eat some of your coconut candies for dessert. So, you can stop hidin' 'em under your thigh now."

"You make me so sick Terry. How you know I got candy under my thigh anyhow?"

"Cause yesterday when we went to Paris, France and you got out in Savannah to pump the gas it was stuck to you. You know you hate sharing up that candy. And me yo best friend and all."

"All right, we can have a little piece for dessert. Sho hope we don't run into no rain on the turnpike."

"It's always raining on the turnpike Missy, you know that. Maybe we ought to take 95."

"That's a thought. Ooh my, my, my, we coming up on a Stuckey's already Terry; look there goes the sign."

"I see it. Get your pecan log at Stuckey's. It's not as good anywhere else."

"Sure ain't. You not gone doze off this time, are you? Cause a long-distance driver need to hear people talk to her. Oh no! Armadillo crossing the road. Looks like he hit! Watch out."

BAM! The whole car rocked. It always does that when you hit an armadillo. It only makes a little bump when you squish a raccoon or a possum. And you get a little wiggle when you get one of those little turtles. But an armadillo -- it shake, rattle and roll the whole car. When it shook, I reached over to Terry, so she wouldn't fly out the window. My mama always does the same thing to me. "Hold the boat sugar, water don't tip my child' over." That's a crazy thing to say, huh, but mama says over and over and every time.

"Hold the boat Terry, water don't tip my child over."

Terry giggled. She has a strange giggle. She giggle like the ghosts on the horror show. Like this hehhe, hehheh, real quiet and deep like. Hehhe, hehheh.

"How you gone keep me from flying out the window with one hand, drive and all?"

"I don't know, Terry. I guess when you reach your hand out like that you just believe you can hold somebody. Did you put on clean panties?"

"I always put on clean panties when we go traveling Missy, you know that."

"Well, I have to ask. I couldn't very well let you fly out the window with dirty panties on, your mama will have a fit at the hospital, if they told her they rescued you in dirty drawers."

"Yeah, she would. Missy, when we get married, what happens?"

"What you mean Terry?"

"I mean do we have to kiss the boy?"

"Terry! He'll be a man then. Maybe then we might even like them"

"You think our mamas and daddies kiss?"

"I saw my people doing more than that. Hold the wheel. You got it good don't ya? Daddy's toes were wiggling like this and mama keep saying - 'yes, wiggle for me baby, wiggle daddy.'"

Boy, did we laugh. When me and Terry laugh it just lasts forever and ever. We get loud and we laugh until we crying. Then we breathe hard and laugh some more.

"Terry, I want to be a TV reporter. Wear some of them Sears and Roebuck suits and ask people all kinds of questions."

"Not me. I'm going to be a president of a company that makes toys. That way no matter how old I get, I'm going to have all the toys in the world to play with. Look at that sign, they put a new hotel in this pitiful little town?"

"Everybody need some place to cheat on his wife, Terry."

"Who you heard say that?"

"I hear your daddy tell my daddy that. Now you got a mama and a sugar mama. Your daddy say she sweeter than sugar water and brown like molasses."

Terry closed her eyes. She always do that when she wants to cry harder than she wanna show. I played like I didn't see her. Sometimes my mouth hurt people feelings. My daddy always tell me to keep an eye on my tongue.

"Look Terry. Your sugar mama just happen to be on the turnpike too. We gon' pull up next to her and throw our shoes at her car. Come on take your shoes off."

We hurried up and took our shoes off. Then when I pulled up right next to that raggedy car of the scarlet heifer, that's what mama called her when daddy told her the story; anyway, I pulled up next to Miss Scarlet Heifer and said; "hey sugar mama." Then we threw the shoes right in her window. She was so scared her wig twisted lopsided on her head. Then me and Terry laughed forever and ever.

"Ooh Missy look at them clouds. It's gone take us longer to get to Texas."

"Yeah I guess so."

"You want to eat now. We been on the road at least four hours now."

"Time flies when you heading out of town."

"Yeah, but don't it drag when you coming back?"

"You know what Terry, I'm going to tell my people to change my name to Dianna -- like Dianna Ross."

"Why? Yo name bother you?"

"Yeah. Make me sound old. Come on you change yours too. You can be Diahann like the lady real name on Julia."

"Yeah. Then we can make up our own signing group, we can be the other Supremes."

"You so crazy."

"Missy can we stop at a rest station. I got to tinkle really bad."

"I told you to go before we left. I always tell you that and do you listen. Head hard as the bricks on the school house. A hard head makes a pissy behind, you know?"

We didn't get to a rest station for another, I'd say ten thousand miles. I'll teach Terry 'bout raising her skirt to me and knocking on wood first too.

"You didn't have to make me hold it on purpose Terry. You can sho be evil when you want to. Now let's go. We ought to get back on the road. It's starting to get dark. You didn't drop the keys, did you?"

"Naw, I got 'em. We might as well finish that Kool-Aid while we ride. Still look mighty cloudy, don't it?"

"Downright nasty. Where we at now?"

"Terry, didn't you see the sign back there. 'WELCOME TO CALIFORNIA'!"

"Oh no! We missed our exit, didn't we? California?!"

Poor Terry, don't she know you get to California before you get to Texas coming from North Carolina. She's pretty and she my best friend, but sometimes she ain't too bright.

"MISSY REYNOLDS . . . MISSY . . . "

"Yes daddy . . . "

"Get on in this house girl. Don't you see that storm coming? Who's that out there with you?"

"Terry daddy."

"You come on in here too. I'll get you home after the rain. I done told you two about playing in that old car. Thing ain't moved in almost a year. All these dolls 'round here and you play in an old car."

What daddy don't know is that car take us everywhere and back. Me and Terry look at each other and laugh.

"Missy tomorrow let's go to Alaska."

"Yeah and play in all the snow.Come on, let's go in my mama room and get dressed for the ball tonight."

We gathered our shoes out the yard, ran through the porch door, being careful not to let it slam behind us and headed to mama's closet. I had already decided I would be Cinderella. Terry better not say a word about it.

Sweet Bird
Defiance

I t had to have been two years since Jacob'd been home. I can't say I was too shocked to see him, hell; Idella started doing her anxious cleaning 'round about I reckon 4 or 5 o'clock yesterday morning. She had done mopped that kitchen for the fourth time before I asked what was troubling her so.

"I can't reach Jacob and he ain't called since day 'fore yesterday. That ain't like him."

Idella was worried and worried something fierce too. So, she cleaned and I sat out on the porch trying hard to be out of her way. Didn't work though, 'fore I knew it she was sweeping' down the porch and stacking up newspapers including the one I was trying to read. Rather than say anything I moved on over to my spot under the tree and hollered for ole Nate to come on out and play a couple hands of wit' me. Idella kept sweeping.

"Awright woman, you done swept every piece o' board in that house. Could be the boy on a field trip. Or he might be with his woman. But even if it is something wrong you sweeping dirt from one pile to another ain't gone make it better."

"And you playing cards is? I'm gonna put dinner on. You know full well, Jacob call every Sunday morning before church; and he ain't called."

"Idella Stewart that don' mean nothin' wrong with the boy."

Finally, Nate rolled on out his shack looking like an old broke down tree limb. Seeing him like that before, I knew he'd slept on that raggedy couch o' his again. He took to doing that on the regular since his heart died 'bout five years ago. Guess sleeping in an empty bed hurt worse than sleeping on a couch a foot shorter than him. We played a few hands and got to reminiscing on our younger days. All the while sipping on the best sweet tea to cross a man's lips and tearing up them apple turnovers Idella sat in the window sill to cool. Just as we got a good laugh going 'bout the time a possum fell through the outhouse roof while Nate was handling his business, I saw a car I didn't recognize pull near the house. Jacob and a white boy climbed out.

"Della, Della!" I hollered into the house, "Your missing child done wandered home. Come on out here woman."

"Uncle Boy. You ain't got a day older than the last time saw you."

"You still cain' tell a lie without laughing. What's this here you got with you?"

Before Jacob could tell me who the white boy was, Idella was swinging on his neck. Kissing him and touching all over him like she was making sure he was breathing. Jacob just braced his self and stood there, real quiet, knowing his aunt well enough to know nothing he could say was going to stop this inspection. The woman checked behind his ears. Can you believe that? What she looking for – ticks?

"Jakee baby, I been worried straight foolish. I been calling you since yesterday. Where you been? How you been? You eating proper? Are you hungry? Can . . . ?

"IDELLA! Woman let the boy talk. Jesus Christ, woman it ain't like you got to change his diapers no more."

The white boy thought that was funny. He sure was a sight – earring in both his ears. Right pretty little square diamonds. Skull cap that sat up kind of high. T-shirt big enough for me and Nate to get into with him. And his jeans, hanging off the bottom of his hips, which was a fight in and of itself cause he didn't have much in the butt area. Della went to lookin' him up and down right crazy like. Then she straightened up her stance and went to talking to the white boy – but talking to Jacob all at the same time.

"I know any properly raised young man knows you take off your hat in the presence of a lady and certainly the seeing of his drawers ain'tsupposed to be attractive. So, I'm reckonin' he gone pull up his pants. Now Jacob baby, are you awright?"

"I'm fine auntie. I'm well. I didn't mean to worry you. I had a black history month program at school – then I just decided to come home for the weekend."

"What's troubling you baby? I see it all in your eyes."

I motioned for Jacob to come on over under the tree. If a woman gone force you to spill your thoughts, you might as well be in a comfortable place to do it. I dealt the cards amongst the three of us and laughed watching the white boy taking in our card room. It certainly wasn't nothing like I know he'd seen in a night club. It was simply some crates, a couple pallets strapped together and some rickety old chairs. And our li'l area didn't sit in no room with a lotta music, flashing lights and beer signs. No sir, our decoration was a big pecan tree and Della's yellow curtains flying through the window carrying the smell of Sunday dinner. It confused the boy – I could tell it did.

Nate stared at Jacob rather odd. "Boy what is wrong with your hair?"

"I'm locking it Mr. Daniels. Dread locks."

Nate smiled, "well awright then – if that's what you say."

Della wasn't gon' let her question go unanswered no matter how hard we talked trash in the middle of the card game. "I asked you what's troubling you Jakee. I sho would like an answer."

"This young man – uncle, auntie, Mr. Daniels is Paul Lesko, he's a student of mine. After school, yesterday he and some of the others started a whole comedy routine about water cannons during civil rights demonstrations."

"Laughing?" Idella grabbed hold to her heart like hearing that tore something in her.

"Naw auntie. Not even, just laughing. I mean standing on the chairs cracking jokes, rapping jokes about it. I thought – my God is that kind of pain funny."

Nate got up from table grabbing his glass. He poured out the tea and reached beneath the table to pour a real drink. Just hearing water cannons made some scars tingle on me. Hearing that children nowadays laugh about it made the making of the scars hurt worse.

"So, Jacob, what'd you bring him here for?"

"I came home because I needed to step into my history again. I don't want to ever become like them. He, well he wanted to see where I came from."

"Jakee where you come from ain' really 'bout a place."

"I know that auntie. That's why I had to come back here. To hear somebody remind me of that."

Nate seemed to have drifted away. While I tried to pretend like I didn't know where his head was, I really did. For a quick moment, we looked at each other. Nate had that tired of white folks look on his face.

"You remember it don't you James? Dr. King was on the radio for days on end. We was all full of his words. Tired of being done wrong cause you was black. Then come one Friday morning . . . Mamie Perkins up at the department store shopping, and the white lady with that bright red up-do told her she couldn't buy the last pair of jeans. Said she couldn't buy 'em for no nigga chile cause a white boy might need 'em more."

I laid my card hand on the table. "Me and Nate had only been in town maybe a week before it happened. Ms. Perkins, her children and a whole bunch of people lined up around the store. I don't think we ever really knew what happened. But before we knew anything, people were locking arms and promising not be moved and there was a line of the meanest looking white men I ever saw in my life. And there we were. Defiant. Mamie Perkins and her black children were going to get those jeans. We weren't gone move 'til they did. Then white boys started moving in on us like a wall. We stood there in the faces of hate.

Then one of them walked up to this pretty little girl, no bigger than a gnat and spit in her face,knocked her down. Bodies came from everywhere. Seems like we was fighting for hours. Cops became dogs, dogs became water, water became bodies and blood and a whole lotta screamin' and cussin."

Nate's hands were shaking as he picked up the story, and he was rubbing them something crazy, like doing that was gone help him not feel that whole day again. "It didn't feel like water though. Oh, my God, I couldn't 'imagine anything like that. Never did I expect to feel something like that. But that feeling of pounds and pounds of water on your skin . . . "

The white boy's anxiousness to understand was still sprinkled in his stupidity. "Just what did it feel like and why couldn't you just run or fight back? Man, I would've been dropping them fools like nothin." Would you believe this boy had the nerve to stand up and show us how we should have tried to weave and bob? Weave and bob in the middle of mean dogs trained to eat black folks and water coming at you at 300 pounds a second.

"Son you ran, of course you did. Or at least you tried to. You fought with whatever you had, whatever you could get your hands on. But that water. That water was like thousands of little knives digging into your skin and then scraping it. It was something powerful; I watched it rip holes in people. "

"That wound still fresh, huh James." Idella pulled me next to her rubbing my arms. I still keep 'em covered under long sleeves.

"Too fresh now that I'm re-living that day. I didn't even know my skin was gone until Nate pulled me into an alley and we started running like hell. We went diving across this fence and there was that tiny girl the man had spit on. She was sitting next to a garbage can trembling and crying something fierce – naked – not one stitch of clothes on her body."

"Naked Paul. The water you and your friends laughed about, tore her clothes clean off her body. Imagine that. Just think about it, outta nowhere you in a concert – it's thumping man and one move leads to a whole incident. Outta nowhere thousands of pounds of water hit your body and knock you 25 feet from where you were standing and when you look down you realize your clothes are gone and you see blood and can't figure out where it came from. It's just water, right, just water. I hope this is starting to feel real for you man. Because I gotta tell you – you kids scare me. Not because of that thug foolishness, but because of this stuff that you take so lightly."

I could see the white boy still didn't get it. Ain' that something. When you really sit down and think 'bout it, them same ole mean white men would round up boys like Paul and kill 'em too for trying to even look like something Black. But, we kept talking. "She was only 16 years old. Nate took off his shirt and put it on her – cause my shirt was soaked in water and blood. We took off running again to a church - about what, man– seemed like five miles down the road."

Idella's eyes started tearing up. "They had to carry me most of the way. And the whole time I just kep' crying. James said, 'look here li'l bird, you know any songs'. I just cried. He said 'I'm gone sing you something. I can't really sing though.' And Nate was yelling something that sounded funny . . . ."

"I tell you what I was yelling Della. This ain't no damn time to sing boy. We can move faster if she run on her own. Run man run."

"Now I knew you was saying run, run. Bill started singing Amazing Grace. And every once in a while, he'd stop singin' and say 'hush crying li'l bird and sing with me."

"Nate man, I was hurting. Her weight on top of mine, both of us. Me not breathing right cause I was talking and singing while I was running. But I knew if I put her down they'd kill her for sure."

"When me and Nate and James got to the church everybody's people were there. My mama just grabbed me from James and cried."

Later that night we found out Mamie Perkins wasn't gone need them jeans no more. Them mean crackers killed both her boys. Two months after all of that I married Idella. She was 12 years younger than me. I had to teach her how to love a man. Fortunately, she already knew how to take care of one. We saw a whole lot of hate over the next few summers. It come right to our front door more times than we would have liked it to.

Funny thing really – the more hate we overcome, the harder we loved each other. Nowadays folks break up cause they cain' pay the bills or cause somebody put on weight. Hard times ought to make you love harder, easy days are for enjoying easy love and change is a chance for me to love you like new. I told Jacob and all of them right there under that tree, these young people ain' got no love for themselves, no respect for themselves – so they cain' really love and respect nothing and nobody else. That's my take on it. Sure, some folks might disagree and they welcome to.

Idella took a deep breath and tried again to drive home why him laughing at somebody's pain cut harder than being stripped and spit on. "Paul, you know what sugar? There's a whole lotta of what you was laughing at living on my husband's skin and in what I see even to this day when I close my eyes at night. Life goes on; yes, it does, on and on. And I guess I cain' expect you to understand how I feel. But I do expect you to not laugh at where I been and what I been through, unless I'm laughing too."

Nate didn't 'preciate the boy's ignorance. "And ain't nan damn one of us laughing. You got some nerves laughing. Maybe if I strung your skinny ass on up that tree right now . . . "

It all had come to close to home for Nate. He had a right to be mad like he was. White boys had cussed him, cut him, spit on him, shot at him, lynched folks he knew, called him every foul name that could come to mind. Now he stood looking in the face of one laughing at what he'd lived through. Part of me wanted to see him strung up in that tree. Part of me knew too that it wasn't gon' stop the ignorance already living in him.

Idella, after awhile, filled up big old plates of black eye peas and ham hocks with the moistest buttermilk cornbread she had done made in a long time. I built a small fire in the kettle to keep the gnats and 'squitos away from my plate and everybody else's. You know how when you first get into your plate everybody get quiet? Well it was then that the white boy finally asked something that might not have gotten him killed.

"I guess we laugh about it cause we think it can't be us. But I gotta ask myself what if it was me? What if it really was me?"

"Tell him Jakee – what is it was him? Just like me and your auntie told you."

"You stand up and no matter how they knock you down, how often they knock you don – you get up, you stand up and you live. You raise a family that knows where and what they've come through and you tell them surviving and succeeding are the only options."

It's been a long time since I'd heard it. And I believe that lesson with every fiber of my being. Still it's easy to think you've learned something when ain't nobody around but you. It's quite a different thang to tell somebody they been ignorant – then help 'em understand why.

Jacob and Paul spent the weekend and when it was time for them to head home, Idella loaded the boy's car with plastic containers full o' food, cakes, pies and a whole lotta stuff he won' gone use. I think he felt better about the things that were troubling him. Ain't it something? Sometimes you need to step back in order to step forward; 'specially when moving forward means what's behind you may not be respected or for that matter even believed.

Idella gave Jacob instructions on how to warm the food. Tried to slip him some money and begged him to cut off his hair. Finally, I pulled her on in the house. Hell, the boy had been trying to leave for an hour before I did. Around about eight that evening, there was a special report on the news. In this day and age, they found a Black man, in his late teenage years, hanging from a tree outside a community college. It happened about four towns away from us. It said, a group of five white boys had been arrested. Lord, have mercy. The hairs in my scars stood on edge. Idella just cried. For the first time, in a long time, I made sure all the doors and windows on the house were locked. I pulled my woman into my arms on the couch, and said, "Sing wit' me li'l bird." And so, we sang the first verse "Amazing Grace"; that's when Jacob called to say they made it home safe. 'Della leaned back on me, and hummed, and hummed, and hummed.

Happy Birthday Baby

The reds and oranges reached to the sky. Crackling, popping, black and graying wood meets it death. Heat shoots forth blanketing the room, like a child being tucked in for the night. And I sit at its threshold shivering. Despite the wood that loses its life for me, I still sit shivering and wiping away the thoughts that invade me. Engulf me. Cool me in the heat of the fire.

This room is so much of me. A mass of juices and skin, I sprang forth, from my mother's wrenching womb here. A woman of 70 with red hair cradled me to her bosom even before my mom. She did the same to all the babies whose parents could not afford the luxury of a hospital in 1963. 1963, the year of my awakening. Now, 30 years later, I come back to my birth to decide on a death.

My mother is a beautiful woman. I am often reminded of the opinion that she and I share the same look. I have not seen this. I am taller. She is of a lighter complexion than me. She has a face that smiles forever. I have one that warns you to find hospitality in other places. She was a good mother and remains one. I, well, I am not yet a mother. Though the application, haphazardly, has now been handed to me.

"I have something to tell you. I'm just not sure how to." That's what I told him, hoping, praying, he would just guess.

"Well, just tell me. You tell me everything else."

"I know. It's just, well, I'll figure out how I should tell you and then I will."

"What is it. Just what is it?"

And I said nothing. Clenched between my hands, the receiver felt like lead. Silence, like a thick fog, filled the air. The intensity of his breathing revealed his dwindling patience.

"What is it?"

"So how was your day?" Stupidity was the name of that question. But attempts to cut short such conversations are usually mindless.

"Are you pregnant?"

The thick silence choked me.

"Yes, I am."

"How long?"

"How long?"

"How far along are you?"

"About eight weeks."

"Didn't you have a period last month?"

"It only lasted half a day."

"You sure?"

"Yes, I'm sure!"

"And?"

"And, what are we going to do?"

"You know how I feel. We've talked about this before. When are you going to have it done?"

That was it. No discussion. No negotiating. Just it. It's like driving in Florida, ten miles of beautiful sun, and a sweet breeze, can be dashed from nowhere with a quick and forceful downpour. Then, that's it. The sweet breeze plays with the sun again. For me, at this moment, it was forceful rain in which I played.

It seems so odd. The photographs carry the history of me and this old home. The Easter photos from 1969. That was the year that, out of a quick infusion of curiosity, I attempted to flush my white straw hat with pink and yellow ribbons down the toilet to see if it would go down smoothly. A snapshot of my kindergarten graduation lay propped against the wall. Everyone always inquires about my tears on that picture. Honestly, I don't know why I was crying; but years ago, I developed a reason for the tears and now, well, now it's the answer even my parents give . . . MY FEET HURT! Reflecting on the memories, the love, the forever of these pictures; I can't help but to imagine the snapshots of my child and wonder what kind of impact they might have on her, or, on him.

"What if I'm not blessed like this again? I'm 30, this might be my last chance." Dammit you better understand. My last chance. MY LAST CHANCE. I had hoped the words would, like the bright, brutally sharp edge of a sword, cut through his wall of practicality. Always remember, hopes are thoughts with no grounds or reasoning.

"You're young," he countered. "There's still time. You don't need this now."

"I don't. No. Actually, the truth of the matter is . . . you don't. It's inconvenient for you. Not part of your little five-year plan. Don't put the burden of inconvenience on me!"

"Calm down. And what does that mean?"

"What?"

"Burden of inconvenience."

"It means you're trying to make it seem like I'm the one who can't handle the consequences of this thing. But you're really worried about how inconvenient it's going to be for you."

"Listen. We've talked about this. I'm not going to argue with you."

"And we've talked about you wearing condoms too. I should've argued with you about that."

"Look. You know how I feel. But it's your decision. Whatever!"

"Whatever?!"

"Whatever."

"I guess I should expect that from someone that lusts for me, but doesn't love me."

"Look! There's no need to go through this. Maybe whatever wasn't the right word. But you know I can't do this right now. Maybe if things were different . . . "

"If you weren't sleeping with two women . . . "

"What?"

"Nothing."

"What are you going to do?"

"I don't know. If I do this, get rid of it, it'll be for you. But tell me something?"

"What?"

"Do you love me?"

"What kind of question is that? You know I have feelings for you. There's something very strong between us."

"That's everything except what I asked. You can be clear on not wanting me in this condition, but you can't be clear on how you feel about me? What is that? Do you love me?"

"You should know that."

"I don't assume to know what someone, especially a man feels. You know what happens when you assume things. You make an ass out of you and me."

"Just let me know what you decide!"

"That depends on you being open with me. Do you . . . never mind. Fine. It'll be over in a couple of days. Then what?"

"You mean between us?"

"Us. Now there's an interesting term."

"Why?"

"Us usually implies two people. Most of the time, I feel like I'm the only one involved in us. You can't say you care. Or you love. Or I think about you. I miss you. If I'm a burden to you just tell me."

"Why are you bringing this up? You know, right now . . . . I just can't tell you those things."

"BYE!"

I never understood why I fall for extremely logical and ever evasive men. It's the two things about people, in general, that I have the hardest time dealing with. People like that, especially men, don't understand that everything is not cut and dry. Drives me crazy. Keeps me intrigued. That's the problem. That's why I'm so in love with someone I haven't even known long enough to spit at.

Every day, growing up in this house, I heard my folks say I love you. Even when they were fighting. Why can't I have that? Once I said, to an old love, "you know I really am crazy about you." He said, "Yeah, you're all right too." All right. That's a world away from crazy about you.

Would the crying stop soon? Would there be any pain afterwards? How am I going to handle it? What kind of fool am I? Could I really do this? Especially not knowing if he has any real, spokenfeelings for me. Am I still going to want him? How could I still care about him, when he's asked me to turn down the best job I could ever have? To tell God, thanks but no thanks, for giving me one of your greatest blessings.

Leaving home, your first home, is always hard. Harder when you're visiting. All those memories cloud you. Everyone fusses over you. I always cry. This time I'm leaving behind an even bigger part of me. And I'm scared. I know that heaven is home to a forgiving God; but I feel like I've laughed in His face. Maybe he'll remind me of that by never blessing my womb again.

"How you doing?"

"Fine."

"Everything go okay?"

"Yeah. You sound tired . . . "

"Haven't had much sleep. I've been thinking about you."

"I TOLD YOU I WOULD DO IT!"

"You're mad at me?"

"Yes and no. I don't know."

"I know you didn't want . . . "

"What I want, wanted, was for you to change your mind. I want you to be open with me no matter what. That's the only thing I've ever asked of you. Why get involved with someone, if you can't discuss the involvement? I love you."

"Don't say that."

"Oh. Okay. Bye."

"Wait."

"What?"

"I'll come by soon, okay?"

"Soon. For you that could mean next week. Whatever. I'll be here crying." And I was crying. And I was in pain. And I still wanted him. And I hated him for not being with me, always too busy, even now. And I prayed for forgiveness repeatedly. And I still can't get this picture out of my mind. It's one of my mother holding me on my first birthday. In the middle of the balloons, streamers and other party fare, she held me, and tears rolled down her cheeks. Happy, happy birthday baby.

There's Far Too Many Of You Crying

"Come on ma stop hitting me now."

"Who in the hell do you think you are? Huh? Big man huh?"

"Stop it ma. Stop it!"

"I work my butt off for you boy, you never need for nothing, and I have to put up with this. One thing after another. Acting like some fool hoodlum. Tell me to stop it. You stop it!"

"Come on ma, I'm bleeding. Ma!"

"Scaring me. You don't know what you doing to me boy."

"Don't make me hit you ma!"

"Hit me! Hit me? Boy, I'll kill you in here. Sit down."

"Man, I'm pulling up."

"You don't put your butt in that chair boy, they'll be pulling daisies up off your grave. Sit down!"

"You all hitting on me and shit."

"What did you say?"

"Nothing"

"What is wrong with you boy? Got me scared. Mad. Crazy. Where do you get this this this foolishness? Stealing cars; for what Darrell? Why you stealing cars? You drive mine more than I do. What is going through your head?"

"Ah, ma, it's just fun. Something to do."

"Don't give me that bullshit boy. Playing football is something to do. Every time I turn around you're into something. Why don't you just kill me?"

"Here we go again."

"Naw, we're not going again. I don't even want to look at you. I'm going to bed. Don't leave this house."

"Come on ma, there's a pa . . . ."

"I SAID DON'T LEAVE THIS HOUSE. SHOULD I SAY IT IN YOUR LANGUAGE? CHILL IN THE CRIB -- DOG!"

"Tripping."

I still collect pieces of his clothing. I've done that every year since his birth. My baby boy's time capsule. These last couple of years, I find myself rejoicing when I choose a piece of clothing to save and it's not covered in blood. I've found everything in his pockets, rubbers . . . knives . . . bullets . . . little plastic baggies, empty, should I be thankful . . . joints. When I confront him, it's word for word. Then I turn around and he's my little boy again. Begging me to make homemade ice cream. Teasing me, and searching the house for birthday and Christmas presents. Making me homemade cards for Valentine's Day. Lord, I can't stand him anymore. I love him with everything in me . . . but I can't stand him.

Fights, stealing, girls calling at two and three in the morning, cussing at anybody he feels like. I didn't raise THAT child. So where is the one I did? I never know what's coming next. Every time the phone rings at work, I shiver, my heart starts racing, sweat starts pouring. I wait for that phone call. Darrell's been hurt. Darrell was killed. Darrell. Darrell. Darrell. Why can't he see it like I do?

"Yo, ma . . . "

"Don't talk to me like that. Respect it or not, I'm still your mother."

"I give you much respect, ma."

"Thank you. It's nice to know you breaking my heart with respect."

"See, come on ma, don't be doing that crying thing. Come on ma."

"Just leave me alone Darrell."

"Ma, I ain't crazy. I ain't gon' do nothing dangerous. It ain't like I'm selling drugs or nothing."

"No. But you're using them."

"What?!"

"I've seen the bags, the weed in your room Darrell. I'm not stupid you know."

"Why you all up in my room?"

"Boy don't question me, this is my house, your tired ass just visiting until . . . "

"Until what ma . . . you think I 'm some jail bound thug don't you?"

"I don't know Darrell, but I know I'm scared of you. Go fix yourself something to eat. I just want to be by myself for awhile."

"You just go sit in here and cry, like always. I'm tired of you crying 'bout me all the time ma."

"So, we even then. Cause I'm tired of you giving me reason to."

"Ma, I ain't never hurt nobody. All right, all right, I smoke a joint now and then . . . "

"And cocaine?"

"Naw that ain't me. I might stick a bag in my pocket when nine questioning somebody."

"Oh, they don't question you?"

"Not most times. I'm always the youngest looking thing around. Chilling in the background, you know, they think I'm just a wanna be."

"Are you? Is that what you wanna be?"

"You don't understand it, ma. You can't get wit' what it's all about."

I can't get with what it's all about. The boy hanging out with boys who have no fear for life. If it ends tomorrow, that's all right, they're going out with a bang. No, I can't get with kids killing each other. Babies selling drugs to babies. I can't get with the fact that I'm losing my son to that world and I don't know how to save him. I can't just rock him to sleep anymore. A warm bottle of formula is not going to feed whatever that need in him is.

"I don't want to lose you Darrell."

"You talking whack ma."

"Can't you just talk to me, without using all of that?"

"You're talking crazy ma."

"I love you boy. If I lose you, I'll lose my mind. You don't have to be doing anything dangerous to end up in danger or dead."

"Ma, I could walk out the door and get hit by a truck. I wasn't doing anything dangerous but – hey - POW!"

"Don't take your life so lightly baby. You're so special to me."

"Most of the time I don't even think you like me."

It's strange to hear him speak the truth, that truth anyway. Watching him fiddling with the fragrance bottles on my dresser, I can't help but remember how curious he was as a child. But he's not more than a child now. I wonder if it's curiosity that leads him to do things that he doesn't need to do. The boy parked my car to go with a bunch of boys to steal another car. I don't . . . excuse me . . . I can't get with that.

"Come here baby. Come sit here with me."

"Come on ma. I ain't a baby anymore."

"I said come here. What's wrong with you Darrell? What are you going to do next? I can't take to much more. I know about all the stuff you don't tell me Darrell. The gun. The fights. I know. I even know about the times they picked your butt up for questioning and didn't call me. Look at me Darrell."

"What ma?"

"Does what I'm saying to you matter at all?"

"Ma, it's just the way we roll now. Like when y'all use to do your whatever whatever."

"Baby, I'm telling you that I think you're going to be dead in the next year, because of how you rolling. I'm telling you I don't want that to happen. I'm telling you, that you are my dog, my child and Darrell the way I fear for you now, it would be nothing for me to kill you just to know you went with love."

121

"Ma, what you talking 'bout? My dogs got my back all the time. Ain't nobody gone take me out like a sucker. That's why I got a gun, I'm a man ma."

"Gun makes you a man. A man fights toe to toe, anybody can pull a trigger. You're a punk, all your friends are punks. I don't want to lose you Darrell, but I'm not gone watch you die either."

"What you saying ma?"

"I don't know baby. But I know something's got to give. Hold my hand."

"What?"

"Hold my hand. Lord . . . "

"Stop that ma, don't be praying over me. I ain't dead."

"Give me your hand back. Lord, you know my heart and my fear in this. In the name of Jesus protect him. Amen."

"It's gone be all right ma. I'm just hanging out, I promise you that."

I pray harder for Darrell now than I ever did. He still cares and I work that nerve as much as possible. I figure if he still cares, he can't be completely gone. Still, I know danger loves a curious eye; and Darrell has always been a curious child.

Tears Of A Clown

A circus of emotions lay about the big top. Anger mulled in the torn curtains that now lay scattered at the foot of the window. Torment clothed the oak dining table that once was decorated by a green-lace trimmed table cloth. A table cloth shredded and distributed in various areas of the big top. And the chord of mayhem played in our heads, as we noticed in disbelief that the elephant had placed his size 13 shoes through the VCR. The only thing more shocking than that was to see that he had used his massive trunk to topple the couch, the ottoman, the shattered glass coffee table. He had used his massive trunk to break through the TV screen, and even worse to shatter the crystal punch bowl that Aunt Jane got from Mama Mae who got it from Grandie who got it from Auntie Reen who some say got him from a white lady when she bought her freedom. But history was only as important as the present developing right now. The big top, now the circus of her life, lay scattered before us. Like children, marveled by the clowns, the animals and the magic acts, we stood speechless – almost catatonic. It was not the first time we had seen his wrath and it would not be the last.

But I held my tongue remembering the words that I had told her weeks before. "I think he's going to kill you. I think you should leave him and I think you should realize that if he kills you, killing your kids would mean nothing."

She begged me to understand that he just sometimes became a different person; for the most part he is the gentle soul that I first met – she would tell me that repeatedly. He is the gentleman that has joined she and I for dinner. He is the sweet minister, with profound statements that amaze. His latest statement, as it were, sent a fierce stabbing sheet of ice through every nerve in my body. And it terrified me. The sheet of cold washing through me. The look of disgust and vengeance on her face. Knowing that all of this came about because we had chosen to go the mall instead of a movie. In his mind, we had conjured up a pair of studs to romance us. She was having a lewd, lascivious and obviously freakier affair with the man in his mind, than she was having with the man of the big top. We stood for what seemed like forever just staring at the destruction. Staring at his schizophrenic reaction to non-reality. And I said nothing, because I kept thinking about what I said to her days before.

"I think he's going to kill you . . . but whatever you decide he's your husband and I will be here for you. Even if it's to help you get away." I had said too much.

"I'm not going to clean this mess up. Help me grab some clothes for me and the kids. I'll stay at Angela's house the rest of the week; she's still in New York. I can't believe he did that to my VCR and my TV. I just bought them Moni. I just bought them."

"Don't worry about those. We can replace them, maybe not brand new, but we can replace them." She slowly slid down the wall, grabbing things from the floor, cleaning up what she couldn't clean up. I imagine, she was trying to stop the river of pain that rushed from her eyes.

I pulled her up. "Don't worry about this room. Let's just get some clothes and get out of here before he comes back."

The circus continued in the bedrooms. Like little midgets piled into the makeshift Volkswagen . . . the children's clothes were piled neatly in a bundle on the bed and they had been ripped into pieces. Nothing hung in the closets. Maniacally, the string and tongues had been cut from their shoes. To me, it seemed like he had laughed at what this rape would do to her. Then something happened. I looked in Val's eyes, and the tears turned into billowing flames. Billowing flames shooting from a burning heart, an engulfed soul.

"Val come on now, as stupid as this sounds, you've got to calm down."

"That is the damn problem Moni, I am calm. I am going to get in my car. I'm going to pick up my kids and put them on a plane to their father. Then, I'm going to my storage unit, reach into that top drawer and I'm going to take out my legally registered hand gun and blow that son of a . . . . no, no, I'm trying to stop cussing. I'm going to politely blow the gentleman away. Wherever I find his a . . . no, no, I'm trying to stop cussing. Wherever I find him, is where I'm going to drop him. See, calm and rational."

Before I could respond she was on a dash for the door; a smoke trail of confusion, fear and anger drifting behind her.

"Val, you are not thinking. Lord knows at this point I can see him dead too. But baby you can't do this. Girl are you listening to me?"

"Moni. You are such a rational woman. And yes, I do hear you. But this day, I'm killing his selfish a . . . no, no, I'm trying to stop cussing."

"Val you've got three kids. As much as I love them, if you go to jail or end up dead, I can't do three kids." She continued to storm through the house, re-arranging the disarray into disarray. Not really paying me any mind. "Val," I grabbed her arm, "listen to me. You cannot just storm out of here and go kill somebody. Not even him. They will put you into jail. They will fry you. They do that in Florida you know?"

"He's already killed me Moni. Have you looked at this house? Have you looked at this scar lately?"

Screaming and crying again, she tore apart her shirt. I had not seen the scar lately. But, why would I? Val never wore sexually attractive clothing anymore; it was the reason for the scar. Chauncey methodically poured scalding water about her waistline one night as she lay in bed. The torture coming after his inner turmoil led him to seduce his wife, leave her panting in bed from satisfaction, place a single red rose beside her sweat drenched hair and then trickle the boiled water down on her. She had worn a short t-shirt over her sports bra to the gym, her slim and tight waist exposed for all to see. No one would want to see the scar from a third-degree burn. No I had not seen that scar lately, but I had seen far too many of his others. Including the one before us now.

"I know you're hurting Val. And I'm not going to even tell you that I know what you're feeling, because I don't. But I know that you can't let him pull you down to his level, don't let him take your life and take you away from those kids. You're the only thing they know. You are their center. You are! Stop throwing shit around and listen to me . . . "

"Shut up Moni. Shut up. Shut up! Don't tell me about my kids. What do you think they feel about their mommy? I'm telling them straight up it's all right for somebody to beat you like a wild dog, if they say – sorry, love you – I can't do this anymore. I'd rather go to jail Moni, then to live like this one more day. I've moved three times in the last two months . . . "

"It does you no good to move Val, if you let him in. If you give him a key. If you ignore the restraining order. You can't believe that you can have sex with a mad man to calm him down or keep him calm. This is not calm. This is demonic. And don't think he's not waiting for you to come for him. Think, baby please. You have got to maintain your sanity for me right now. I'm scared Val. Don't jump out of the frying pan into the fire."

"It won't matter Moni; I've already been burned."

Val and Chauncey had met at Miami-Dade Community College. They ended up in an English course together. Val switched to a night class because of her work schedule. We both thought it was kind of cute; the way Chauncey had left cards and single roses with all the night teachers looking for Val. He didn't know her name, but he left a very detailed description with each card. Finally, after about three weeks of cards and roses and no response, Chauncey showed up and waited in a corridor hoping to find Val. He did. From that point on, it was a seemingly normal relationship, exceedingly romantic, almost to the point of sickening. But then I was the one without a man at the time, so anything would have been romantically sickening to me. Val was impressed by him and why not. He was charming, good looking with a teddy bear appearance and smile, and a warm embrace. Intelligent and always willing to engage you in the most interesting conversations. He had a way with children. He had a way with Val.

"Everything that glitters ain't gold." That was Val's Aunt Jane's opinion of Chauncey from the beginning. She had a wisdom of abusive men that we were not aware of. One that Val ignored, but one that I found frightening and intriguing. I couldn't let it go. Val never paid it any attention. She always said it was just an old lady's fears.

"Monica," in the seven years I've known Aunt Jane she's always called me by my actual name. No matter how I begged her not to or explained that I didn't like the name. I am Monica to her. "Valiece don't see that boy for what he is. But I can feel it. He is just as evil as he is sweet. The very Bible says you can't serve two masters and he does and he don't ever know which one is real."

"Auntie, Val says he's the best thing she's ever had. He seems to be good for her. What is it that has you so scared of him?"

"You get a chill in front of him. Before you even see him, you feel him. That's evil. It sits quiet stirring up on the inside and then it tears you up. I know what I'm talking about. I tell you he's going to take her away from you, from me, from them kids and then it's going to be too late."

"Why don't you tell Val?"

"You can't tell a woman 'bout her man. Especially when she figures her man stuff don't stink. When men have head problems, they fix things up really good. They tell you all the right things, cry at all the right times, cook, clean, love you to death. Cause when their evil show up, they know what makes you weak and that's what they use to beat your ass the next time."

I don't think I'd ever heard it put quite that way before. She was right. We don't listen to each other when it comes to our man. We know him better. We feel him better. We got it working better. We never even see that fist slamming into our face. Val has been blind for so long. And the sight that she has finally been given, has taken her to a dangerous place.

Tumbling about the floor we looked like two rug rats on spring break. But I couldn't let her leave in such rage, such pain. This was a dangerous place for her to be emotionally and mentally. We wrestled on the ground and she fought me for control of those keys. Somewhere in the back of my mind I kept asking why didn't you fight him like this. Why? Suddenly I left a gripping about my neck and I was flung across the room. We never saw Chauncey come in. He pulled Val up from the floor by the neck, pinning her to a wall. He held her screaming, "my father which art in heaven, what do I do, what do I do. Lord, I take it." I grabbed a butcher's knife from the kitchen, touching him on the back with it, so that he knew – so that I knew, I would cut him. He dropped her. Val slid down the wall, hitting out at him. Trying to find her breathing again, she gasped for me to run; but I couldn't leave her there. He was going to kill her.

"Chauncey, you need to leave. Get out of here, or I'll call the police." I yelled waving the knife before him. He never even acknowledged me. He fell to the couch and broke out into tears. That was not enough for me. "I said get out Chauncey. Nobody wants to hear your sad story, your twisted version. I want you OUT! NOW!

Val grappled to get up from the floor, slipping back to her knees not once but twice before she finally rose, still trying to get her breathing stable.

"What the hell is wrong with you man? Look at my home. My kids have to come home to this." He never looked up. "Don't you even care? Don't you realize what you've done?"

With his face buried in his hands, he mumbled. Nothing at first, then slowly. "Valiece, I love you, but your friends come between us. I get crazy. I'm sorry. Val, I'm sorry."

Val stared at him. In a split second, something in her demeanor let me know that this was not the last time this circus would be in town. Still, the mess of the present time upon her, she chose to protect herself.

"You're right Chauncey. You are SORRY! You are a SORRY EXCUSE for a man; I don't know why I love you so."

There was victory for Chauncey in the confession of love and Val didn't even know it. She motioned for me and as we headed for the front door, he lunged at Val grabbing her arm. With one quick motion, I landed the knife across his upper arm. He yanked away.

"You see Val. This is what I'm talking about. I just wanted to hold you."

Val ran out the front door; leaning against the car she began to throw up everything that filled her. Four weeks and one more incident later Val and Chauncey were back together. And he had achieved what Aunt Jane feared. Val no longer dealt with her. The kids were safe with their father in South Carolina. Val and I rarely spoke. One of the last times we did, she politely chastised me for cutting Chauncey. I said nothing.

During a sermon one day, I heard the pastor say that there are some battles that you are just not to be involved in. Some turmoil cannot be solved on earth. I think Chauncey's turmoil is of a supernatural nature. I think Val has become part of a dangerous sorority. In Chauncey's world, she ceased being the strong, super-intelligent, independent fighter that I have known for years. When she crossed over, his battle was won; when he needed to beat up on somebody who would not fight back, she was there.

I would call her. She would not talk. I would tell her I pray for her, she would laughingly say, "girl I need it." Her bill collectors would call me looking for her. He was apparently spending all the money on only God-knows-what. Despite his spending habits, she took – I heard - several beatings about bill collectors or as he would call them "boyfriends" calling the house. Finally, I had enough of our relationship. One of us had to let go of Chauncey and since I was not his wife, it had to be me.

Letting go of him, meant letting go of Val as well. That hurt. There were times when the rain would beat slowly against my window, that I would see her battered face or hear her screaming. Then I would call and she would not talk. I let go of Val – finally. You know you can extend your hand to someone but for a time. Then your arm grows weary and tired and eventually falls back into its rightful place. And the thing that you reached for slips away.

It had been a year and I had not seen Val or Chauncey. Aunt Jane saw her only in spells; mainly when she was not bruised and when she was broke – financially - and didn't know where else to turn. When her pride had taken it last breath, she stayed hid and I stopped trying to find her.

What else could I do? Loving her meant hating him meant losing her. But I never said anything. So, for everything I never said Val, Valiece, standing here holding on to this cold, metal hospital rail, know that I will be right here for you. I felt a comforting hand on my shoulder and the nurse urged me to get a cup of coffee or lay down in the nurse's lounge. But I was afraid to leave her again. No, she didn't know I was there. No, she didn't know she was there. But I was afraid to leave her again. As the IV dripped slowly into her nearly lifeless body; I saw her at her wedding singing "You Bring Me Joy" to a man that would destroy her. Nothing could help me comprehend how you bring me joy led to a man stabbing his wife more than 30 times as he made love to her. When the police burst into the house he lay against the headrest next to her bleeding body drinking a glass of water.

For everything I never said Val, let me say this, may you know in your next life that joy need never mean pain. I love you.

Grammy's Pie Cabinet

First of all, I just want to make something perfectly clear; I am not crazy. Yes, I do let my thoughts get the best of me every now and then. But basically, I'm sane. You ever see something, I mean the smallest, most insignificant thing and it has this amazing impact on you. A picture, a doll, a flower, something every day and ordinary, but suddenly, you notice the slightest thing and boom, you're in tears.

When I was a kid, we would spend summers at my Grammy's house in the country. I loved this house, because it represented a whole different world to me. I knew none of the kids on the block went away for the summer and got to pump water, or get water from a well, or use an outhouse or a chamber pot. And I knew none of them got to play dress up with jewelry that was older than their parents like I did. My Grammy had this side room in her house. And this house was made of the oldest and thickest wood I had ever seen, and parts of the roof were made with tin. But the side room, with the wide, blue and white throw rug, was full of hats and dresses and shoes she wore when she was 21 and "co'tin'" as she called it.

And it had an old, small, record player my granddaddy bought for me. I would listen to my records and play dress up until she'd call me to eat, or go into town with them.

I hadn't thought about any of that in years; until . . . Here I am walking through this antiques flea market, not really impressed with anything I was seeing. I'm standing here admiring this serving plate, bowl thing, and I'm thinking, Grammy had one like that. Big and heavy, white with a fading blue floral pattern. It was big enough to sit a medium turkey in. Grammy would pull hers out and load it with cornbread stuffing and giblets or mashed potatoes on holidays. They wanted 20 bucks for it, can you believe that, 20 bucks for the plate, bowl thing. Still, in all my complaining it found its way into my arms. For a moment, I could smell the onions dancing with the giblets in

Grammy's stuffing. That's when I saw it. I drove home frantic and called my best friend Cheryl.

"Cheryl, you won't believe what I saw over in Gadsden today at the antiques flea market."

"It's the middle of the night, isn't it?" Okay, yes, I know Cheryl is an early to bed person, and yes, even at only this hour it was the middle of the night for her.

"No, it's like one or two. Cheryl, a pie cabinet."

"I don't have one. Goodnight."

"Cheryl, no, I'm not asking you for a pie cabinet, I'm telling you I saw one. A pie cabinet."

I could hear her ruffling the covers. Now that I had awakened her, I was sure she would lecture me on respect and consideration for one's time.

"Daante, why is it important to me at 1:45 in the morning, that you found a pie cabinet. What in the hell is a pie cabinet?"

People from up north don't know anything about stuff like that, they're more into breakfast nooks. Why anyone would need a breakfast nook, I still don't understand. But a pie cabinet. That is a necessity. I explained to Cheryl, that a pie cabinet is a piece of history from grandmothers of the south. My Grammy had one.

I loved that pie cabinet. The one in the antique shop made me remember Grammy's. Now the one at the shop was a light colored crippling wood cage, held together barely by rusting nails, and it had the latch that you turned to hold the doors closed. But Grammy's pie cabinet, was a deep beautiful wood brown, it had markings on it, surely put there by the throngs of kids that had come through that house and to me it reached the ceiling.

"Fine Daante, you saw a cabinet that reached the ceiling. You get some sleep, you must be car sick."

Cheryl can be very sarcastic when awakened before time.

"Cheryl, I didn't . . . my cousin and I used to stand in front of that pie cabinet and just look at it. When Grammy made pies, the smoke from the heat would come through the wire mesh that acted like a glass covering to the cabinet. There was something sweet about the way the cinnamon brought out the odor of the wood."

"Are you having a private moment here?"

"All right, I'll walk down memory lane by myself. You can go back to sleep."

"Oh no, you'll just call me back in a few minutes, finish this bedtime story now. Cinnamon and odor and . . . "

Don't you love having friends you can wake up in the middle of the night and know they still love you.

"Yeah. There were times that I would try to open the latch to get to the pies, or the cakes and donuts, whatever Grammy had in it. I never could though. One time, me and my cousin, pulled the chair right up to the cabinet, we had that latch moving. Then there was Grammy, 'somebody gone have some tanned hinds if they don't get away from that cabinet.'

Cheryl finally laughed, "you were a terror as a child too, huh?"

"Funny."

"Why are you making such a big deal out of this thing? It's just a bunch of wood and nails."

"You see that's the wrong attitude. That's probably the same attitude the person had that gave that pie cabinet to the antique shop to be sold. It is so much more than that. It's about home. About finding a piece of home."

It's true, that why seeing a cabinet that would probably blow apart with a strong wind, brought tears to my eyes. You grow away from home. I guess, I told Cheryl, that looking at

Grammy's pie cabinet through the wooden structure in the store, made me realize how less simple things are now. How it was never really about the pies, cakes, cookies or the big bowls and plates that Grammy kept in the cabinet. It was more about how she did all that baking because she loved us. It was about protecting things so that she could give them to one of us one day. That pie cabinet was about storing away the things that made home.

But, can you believe they wanted 750 dollars for that pie cabinet? The thing was falling apart. I could have built a better one myself. The nails were orange with rust. He wanted 750 dollars.

"Antiques" said Cheryl, "are almost always expensive Daante."

"Well maybe I should've looked around some more. Maybe he had a chamber pot for 50 dollars."

"A chamber pot?"

"Yes. It's kind of like a round metal bucket you kept under the bed, so if you had to pee at night, you pulled it out and went."

"In a bucket Daante. God I never knew you were so primitive."

"No, it's just that you're too northern. I bet your father and mother know about things like that."

"So, are you going to get this pie cabinet or not."

"I don't think so. Besides . . . "

"All right Daante. I'll go with you to get it tomorrow. But if I get one splinter, girlfriend, you're on your own."

"Good night good friend."

"Yeah . . . yeah . . . damn pie cabinet, two o'clock in the morning."

E. Claudette Freeman

How about that I'm going to own a pie cabinet. Of course, I'll have to dress it up a little, put some sturdier nails in it. Bad thing about it is, it doesn't go with anything in my kitchen. Good thing about it is, it goes with everything in me.

One Piece Don't Win
This Game

After 14 hours of hectic-on-speed in the emergency room for the second night, exhaustion once again felt like a bothersome and terrible lover – ever present but draining unpleasantly. Every number on every diagnostic and monitoring read the same thing to me, 2238 – the house numbers in my address. This exhaustion made the leather headrest in the BMW I bought myself as a birthday gift feel like a comfy pillow. I thought I would take in the moment of no pages, no stat calls for labs, and no comforting frightened patients. I needed the quiet. I needed the coolness of the air conditioner blowing on my face. I needed a moment – this moment.

The moment wasn't mine to have. "Perhaps," mini-ini-me whispered, "we are just seeing things. After all, through tired and swollen eyes, strange visions are normal occurrences." The voice within and I agreed. We did not see a paper thin, blonde woman, rushing from my front door. We did not see a paper thin, blonde woman, rushing from my front door and climb into a Cherry Red Ford150 parked in front of the empty house next door to me. We – did not see this paper thin, blonde woman, rushing from my front door with her bra in her hand.

Did she not have enough class to put her damn undergarments back on her body? Perhaps they realized that I might actually show up to my own house soon and grabbing it was an afterthought. She messed up my moment – again. The chick I used to be knows something. She knows that the blonde with bra probably has noticed me watching my own house while she frolicked on my brand-new sheets. She probably appreciates the fact that she could apply her salve of seduction on brand new bedding.

My friends think I am obsessed with bedding. One day, I will divulge that the obsession comes from throwing away one set for a new one each time I think I smell her – whomever the her-of-the-week is - in my room. She had a nice back-pack-styled purse thrown across her shoulder. Why couldn't she just put the bra, in her bag? She wanted the neighbors to see it. It was her way of daring them to say something to me. She wanted me to see it. That's what she really wanted - for me to see it. Cool. She won that point – but one point won't win this game.

A tap on my driver's window furthered the intrusion into my moment. Still, I relished the aroma of the hot cup of coffee the caramel colored hand offered as the window eased down.

"You didn't have to watch too long this time I see." He had a warm way about him. Warm enough to temper what should have been a strong cussing. The badge dangling from the lanyard around his neck pushed the strong words I could have spoken down further.

"This time? How do you know this is a "this" time?" I sniffed then sipped the coffee, wishing it had a tad more sugar and cream. I wished it didn't come with the knowledge that someone else was aware of the weekly freak show and its show times in my house.

"Tell you what, step back here to my car with me; and I'll tell you what I know. Plus, I tend to drink my coffee a little on the strong side; you may need to dress yours up a bit. I have a stash of sugar and stuff in the car. I got some cinnamon buns too."

I hesitated. "Just because he's a cop" – mini-ini-me proffered, "doesn't mean he ain't crazy. He just crazy in uniform." Still, after watching the blonde with the bra leave my home, a moment in a police car was a powerful remedy to the image of me accidentally with deliberate intent tripping some 35 times into Mr. Lover Man's body with my favorite butcher's knife, before applying peroxide to clean the wounds. Certainly, as a medical professional, I couldn't allow him to meet God - or satan as it were - with infected wounds.

I popped the door open and pulled the key from the igni-
tion. Sipping the brew that brought clarity to my moment, I
focused on the not quite handsome, but wonderfully well-
stocked officer before me. I climbed into the passenger side
of his service vehicle, taking note of the scanner, the mounted
computer, the cuffs and other accessories nestled in their
respective places. His words came as a bit of surprise to me.

"Two mornings a week, and one night a week, you pull up
in that same spot and watch that house. I noticed it a few times
checking out something else in the area. Then I noticed, after
a certain period of time you'd use your key to access the house
and you always start punching in the code before the door
closes."

"I'm a creature of habit. What can I say?"

"Husband? Or just man?"

"Husband. At this point, I'll reserve judgment on whether I
think he is a man or what kind of man I think he is. How many
times have you seen her leave my house?"

"That's none of my business. I just noticed you grab the
steering wheel a bit differently this morning. Thought you could
use a bit of a distraction."

"And you just happened to have coffee? To distract me?"

"Naw. The coffee was intentional. This is one of your two
mornings. I thought perhaps I could offer an ear. Or, some
advice."

"If you want to offer advice, then I will assume that just like
me – you've seen her leave my house before."

"We both have seen them leave your house before. Haven't
we?"

"We have. We have indeed." I never intended the tears to
fall. I promised myself I was not going to cry about this situation. I knew what was up. I knew he didn't care that I knew. I
knew that even though we had not practiced full disclosure, this

marriage was over and he was still - sadly - the man I married. "I fell for this one line; he used to always tell me. 'Something about you calls out to my potential.' Ha! In my mind, we were going to maximize this collective potential."

"Well. I'm sorry you've had to watch it play out like this. I've seen far too many situations like this end up very violently and tragically. When I realized what you were doing, I thought it best to say . . . ."

His hand against his full lips seemed to warn him to be mindful of his words. The coffee he sipped, as I did, perhaps gave him tactful instructions.

"Officer . . . I'm sorry. We never introduced ourselves. Sadie Lloyd-Shepard."

"Daniel Weathers."

"Officer Weathers. How long have you been watching me, watching them?"

"About four months now."

"I've been watching for six months. Crazy, right?"

"Well, I'm not married – and I'm not a woman in love, so I don't think I can say what's crazy. I will say this, no woman deserves to watch women leaving her home or using her home for, we'll keep it clean and say – seductive indiscretions. Why do you still do it - watch the house I mean?"

I leaned back into the seat of his car, and stared at the rose bush in the new neighbor's yard. She really brought the yard to life. She made me want to give much more attention to land-scaping and creating a personality for my home. I slowly turned to face him. Stern, but warm, he thinks one of us is in danger.

"I think part of me wants him to be the husband I imagined. The husband I've wanted since I was a little girl. Part of me believes that he loves me more than every single one of them."

"Mm. I see. How long have you been waiting for that?"

"Since about three months before we were married."

"But you still married him."

"I encouraged his potential – remember. I thought that was enough to combat what I thought was happening." He shifted in his car and watched something very intently in his rear-view mirror. "Duty calls?"

"A little." He pressed the button on the communication device attached to his shoulder and rattled off some codes. It all sounded extremely official and exciting. I wanted to turn around to see what he saw; somehow, I knew that was not a good idea. "So, Mrs. Lloyd-Shepard, what's your plan?"

"Well, I don't really think I should tell you what I was thinking before you tapped on the window because you would probably either arrest me or commit me. Right now, I'm just going to fix myself a hot breakfast and lock myself in the guest room."

"The guest room?" His question was wrapped in shock.

"Too tired," I was angered as I heard the words resonate in the deepest pit of abandoned love in me. "Too tired. I'm too tired to change the sheets, and clean until the smell of sex I didn't have leaves the room today."

The morning air punched me as I pushed the car door open vigorously. I heard his door open as quickly, and in the press of the moment, I hated this cop. This cop, who had the audacity to show some common, decent concern. This cop, who had the audacity to show some common, decent concern that forced me to face the truth. One point may not win a game, but too many points become offensive. And man, I'm offended.

"Listen, Mrs. . . . ."

"Sadie, please, I still know who Sadie is."

"That's good to know." That caramel hand with only a Mason's ring extended another token of release. "Call me if you need someone to talk to. If you need a lead to resources. I work this area. A lot of the businesses and neighbors know me. If you can't find me tell them I told you to ask for help."

"I don't think he'll hurt me."

"Funny thing, Mrs. I'm sorry Sadie . . . but hurt is already evident. In my opinion he's an expert in how he applies it; and unfortunately, it seems you're becoming immune to how it feels."

His words shook me. His words terrified the mini-ini-me. I never intended to be immune to being hurt. I never intended to be immune to being the other woman, the aggravating side-piece in my own marriage. I held the card in my hand, trembling at the weight of his words. Hurt is already evident, and you're becoming immune to how it feels. I felt myself moving, but it was more like I was outside of me, not there. I stopped just at the entrance to the yard I wanted to landscape; slowly I turned to the left and in our minds (mini-ini-me and mine) I saw the blonde with the bra. I turned to the right and in our minds, I saw the hippy chick with the blue Mohawk. I glanced to the top of the driveway and in our minds, I saw the short girl with the disproportionate breasts. We told ourselves again, "no he wasn't rubbing her belly, he does not have a child out there somewhere that is not ours."

I placed my hand on the mailbox and the tiny squeak it makes when opened seemed to yell, REALLY, WE ARE GOING TO PRETEND LIKE YOU DIDN'T SEE ALL OF THAT! I saw them all in every corner of my yard, peeping out of my windows, waving as if we are friends; yet grimacing like I was the funk in the room. I turned back to Officer Weather's car, realizing I hadn't pulled mine into the driveway. He leaned against the hood of the car, drinking his coffee, watching me. I stood returning his stare. As suddenly as he tapped on my window, he stood in front of me, his hands on each of my arms.

Stern and warm. "Are you okay?" I said nothing. "Would you feel better if I took you to a friend's or a family member's?" I said nothing. "I tell you what . . . I'm going to walk you back to my car and we can figure it out from there." I said nothing. "Can you tell me if you have a weapon – in your purse, in your car, in the house?" I said nothing, but shook my head. "That's a good thing. Will you do me a favor?"

I nodded. "Good. If you want to go inside and get some things and then I can take you somewhere or call someone to come get you, turn towards your front door. That's all I need you to do, turn towards your front door. I will take that as permission to enter your home."

I said nothing. Mini-ini-me screamed, "turn, turn, turn, turn – please turn!" I turned and breathed. I was inhaling and exhaling, but I hadn't breathed in years. I breathed. I turned to my home and breathed.

"I need to take out the trash." I looked at Officer Weathers. The slant of his eyes searching for some semblance of sanity from me.

"Ok. If you feel the need to do that."

I took a step and he did likewise. I felt my breaths. I took another step and he followed. I felt my breaths. I heard the front door open and there he stood. He stood to take my breath away. I felt my breaths, warming within. I smiled at Officer Weathers, and motioned for him to follow me towards the door. "Officer Weathers, this is my husband, Darris. This is the trash that needs to go out."

"Good morning, sir. Can you step outside and have a conversation with me, please?"

His protests were loud. He pled his case for all the neighbors to hear. I tried to walk past him. He blocked me. I breathed. I tried to walk past him again. He grabbed me. I yelled. Officer Weathers stepped up. I waved his flags amidst his demands, tossing the queen size sheets, blankets, and pillowcases out of the window. What dollar store musk-wanna-be was she wearing? And is that a cigar scent I smell? Aw, hell naw. I'd have to leave all the windows in the room open to release her linger.

"Here Darris, take these too, you picked them out." I tossed the pillows, which I'm sure he used for leverage, out the front door, slamming it as he moved to rush towards it."

"I'm sorry, Officer Weathers. I hope that stench didn't hit you. Listen; let's grab coffee sometimes under different circumstances."

One broken window, one pushed cop and one pair of handcuffs; and far too many years of pretending to be blind– one point learned - I don't deserve to live in another woman's essence. I don't deserve to be interference in my husband's life, and in my home.

Seriously, who walks out the door with their bra in their hand? Tasteless.

The Way My Mama Loves Me

T
he trip had taken less time, than Jamie Taylor antici-
pated. As she pulled off the road, she stared at the same
little sign in the hole, that had welcomed tourists, since
she was a child. "YOU ARE NOW ENTERING PELHAM, GEOR-
GIA." She found herself smiling at the memories of her childhood. The times she and her cousins played stickball in the
road. The way the clay dirt felt between her toes. Then there was
the time Kirk had hit the ball into the graveyard. Jamie, being
the youngest was forced to retrieve it. So off to the graveyard
she ran. Brave little soldier, off to fetch the ball.

That incident was more vivid than most of her other childhood memories. When Jamie found the ball, it was in the hands
of an old woman. Kids always said this woman lived in the cemetery and that she was a ghost. To Jamie, she was very much
alive, and she was pretty, smooth. She had brilliant brown skin
with eyes blacker than the big kettle pot her grandmother fried
pork skins in. Yet these eyes were as clear as marbles. You could
see right through them.

This woman. Jamie could remember her so vividly, she wore
a red dress, and a long string of pearls, with a broach made of
pearls and diamonds. Jamie started crying. In her mind, she
could hear that woman's voice clearly, so very clearly. Smooth,
warm and soft. She had touched Jamie's pony tail and told her
how pretty and plump she was. She gave Jamie her first lesson
on accepting emotions as things not always spoken. Yet at only
eight, Jamie did not comprehend the meaning of the words.
"The one you want to love you won't 'til she can't love no more.
But you gotta know l'il bit, that it's alright to love her just the
same." Then she handed Jamie the ball and sent her back to her
cousins.

The memory sent waves of ice through Jamie. Why after all
these years did she remember that? Suddenly, two little girls ran
across the road in front of the car, and Jamie took the moment to

wipe away the tears. As she rolled down the window, and hoped the fresh air would clear her mind; the smell of Pelham sifted through the car. The smell of damp wood, large pots of collard greens and ham hocks, pork roasts and homemade pound cakes; and yes, there was even the smell of an old outhouse. Five years. It had been five years, since she'd been home. It was her mother's phone call that brought her back here.

"Well Jamie baby, put it in gear and get it over with," so she told herself as she headed down Whitehurst Road. this was the part of town where mostly older White folks lived, and it brought an ironic smile to her face to remember that when she was no more than 10, Black folks weren't allowed in this area. For the first time, she could see how warm and family-like these homes looked. Clay bricks and white wood with metal doors, "and even those old ugly chicken weather vanes," Jamie laughed. Then she recalled the conversation with her mother that beckoned her.

Matthew, Jamie's husband answered the phone. The ringing at four in the morning had frightened her.

"Hello." Nothing. "Hello." Still nothing. Then a sudden knowing told Matt to hand the phone to Jamie.

"Hello . . . hi Mama. How you doing?"

"I didn't call for small talk, I want you to come home and bury me. The Lord ready for me now. He's told me."

If she wasn't awake, that statement certainly did the job. She quickly kicked the covers off and sat up in bed. Her voice, her whole body was quivering.

"Bury you. Mama what the h . . . "

Before she could finish the sentence, and as is usually the case with her mother, she interrupted her . . .

"Don't talk to me in that tone. Unfortunately, I ain't got nobody but you; and I need you to make sure they put me in the ground right."

CLICK. SHE WAS GONE!

"What's this about burying somebody?" A sarcastic tone was in Matt's voice. Jamie couldn't blame him. Her mother never liked him. In fact, it was her decision to marry Matt, that had kept her away from Pelham so long.

"Mama thinks she'd dying. She wants me to come home to bury her. Alone, I suppose." She looked at Matt, like a child lost for an answer to a math problem. "Why does she do this to me? She didn't come to my graduation, nor our wedding, and she hates everything I've ever done. Why do I have to bury her?"

Enraged at the thought of burying someone she wasn't even sure she loved. Jamie grabbed her night gown from the floor, covered herself and headed for the kitchen. There it was chocolate cake; the immediate answer to her problem. Matt's arms warmed the lace on her night gown as he pulled her closer.

"Put the plate back and talk to me." He pulled her away from the cabinet and into his arms as he sat down. "This isn't something you have to do. You could just make arrangements from here, and we don't even know if she's really dying."

Jamie rested her head against his. "I don't know Matt. I have no idea why she thinks she dying. All I know is, despite it all, she is my mama. I wouldn't want our sons to let strangers bury me." Knowing he understood she kissed him, and gently stroked his face. "If you'll keep an eye on the boys, I'll leave in the morning."

He returned the kiss and squeezed the hand that stroked him, "if it's what you want, fine, we'll be here."

There it was, Love Street, just ten run-down wooden houses to go. Jamie made a mental note to call home and thank Matt for being there for her. The house still looked the same. She peeked down that path that led back to home. Smoke rose from the chimney; and on the porch of one of the houses that sat on the front of the road was Chayonne. Crazy Chayonne, that's what the kids called her. She was Jamie's great aunt, and a colorful character. Legend had it she could pee in an old-fashioned Coca-Cola bottle without a spill. Jamie had always imagined Chayonne as a beautiful young girl, and a heart breaker. The thought of Chayonne's soda bottle legend amused Jamie and eased the anxiety, the fear, the sorrow that filled her and she drove up the final leg of that dirt road. Miss Millie's collard green garden was in full bloom as were the rows upon rows of various colored flowers that she grew.

As always Jamie's mother was cooking. It smelled like peach cobbler. Something with cheese, probably macaroni and chitterlings. As she closed the car door behind her, she figured it would be strange eating chitterlings. Matt doesn't eat pork, so the only time Jamie ate it, was when she at alone. Every step seemed like such a major one now. Then knocks on the door seemed loud enough to wake the dead. Then there was her mama. Jamie wanted to hug her. Slap her. Kiss her. Cuss her. Run away and hide.

"You lettin' all the heat out. Come on in baby." Bessie Davis reached for her daughter and held her tightly. But just for a few seconds. "It's so good to see you mama. Every time I come home, you're cooking."

"Well, a soul has t'eat. Take you stuff to your room."

Jamie headed for her old room. Every room felt strange. The house seemed to rape her. Room by room. Thought by thought. Stripping away her strength and independence. By the time, she reached the room, she was weak and filled with worry. Buckling to the emotion, she fell across the bed and took quick, short breaths to calm down.

"JAMIE. JAMIE. COME HERE, I WANNA SHOW YA SOMETHING."

Hearing her mother call, Jamie collected herself and headed towards the living room.

"Look here. This is my insurance policy and my arrange-ments. All you gotta do is call Mason's, they'll handle it from there." Bessie never looked up from the papers she had laid on the table before her. Jamie was growing impatient. She could feel her eyes beginning to squench and her rather sizeable nose beginning to flare.

"Mama, why? What?" She was becoming frustrated, and as she started to speak again, Bessie rose and headed to the kitchen. Jamie followed closely.

"I know it's my turn. Can hear the angels calling roll. I'm ready. You might as well be ready to." Bessie seemed so uncon-cerned about the situation. Selfish, so Jamie thought.

"Mama, don't you know you're scaring me. I can't. I don't want to deal with this. You never wanted me to be a part of any-thing important to you before. Why now? Why this?"

Bessie ignored her. Jamie grabbed her arm and pulled her attention away from the pots bubbling on the stove. Angry. Bessie snatched away, slamming a large metal stirring spoon on the counter top.

"Grow up chile! Did ya think I'd live forever for you to ignore! I had to be here to bring you life. The least you can do is be here to see that I meet death."

Jamie fell against the refrigerator as Bessie pushed past her. Closing her eyes to fight back the tears; she grabbed the phone and prayed Matt would be home. There to ease the hate that enveloped her heart.

"Hello . . . hey baby . . . it's me. Yes, I made it safely," then looking to heaven as if to ask God to forgive her for lying; "things are going great . . . "

Her neighbors must have heard the silverware clanging against the plates that night. There were no words to muffle the noise.

"Mama." Then nothing.

"You always were scared to speak yo mind."

"Only to you Mama," she looked up to meet a curious glow in her mother's eyes. "What were you like when you were my age?"

"Strange question child. I was just a plain girl form Pelham, with a new husband and child that kept kicking me from the inside." Bessie's curious glow grew into a cynical twinkle. "You not trying to fin' me in you, is you." With that she pushed away from the table and started clearing the dishes.

"Is there anything wrong with that. I am your daughter." Jamie looked out the kitchen window. The same thick trees still stood there. Miles and miles of woods stood behind those trees. What could be back there? Who could be hiding? What could those woods know?

There to the left stood the old chicken coop. Nothing more than rotting wood, rusting tin and odor now; this chicken coop used to be Jamie's Aunt Paul's opera house. Jamie would sit in the coop among the chickens and droppings and eggs yet to hatch and listen to Paula praise the Lord in song . . . We're marching to Zion. Beautiful . . . beautiful Zion. We're marching over to Zion, that beautiful kingdom of God. And, ooh, the way she could move through Amazing Grace. Hitting high notes so fiercely your heart would race frantically. Then in a split second, hitting a low note so smoothly you felt as though she'd put her arms around you. Jamie never understood why she always cried when Paula sang. But then she would always reason that the old ladies in church were right, "When the Lord moves you, tears need no explanation." Paula killed herself when she was 20. Jamie was only 12. Paula'd gotten pregnant and felt she couldn't sing to the Lord any more. Amazing grace. How sweet the sound.

"You always in a world someplace else. Didn't you hear me talking to you." Jamie turned to face Bessie.

"Naw, I didn't. I was thinking 'bout Paula."

"Paula found a solution to having a child she didn't want. I can certainly understand what she was feeling."

"DAMN!" Jamie whispered, her back to her mother. The scowl on her face seemed to seek an answer to the implication that her mother thought about killing herself instead of giving birth to her. It was a dangerous realization. One that they both ignored.

"I asked about the twins, how they doing?"

"They're growing. Looking more and more like their daddy." The fact that Bessie asked about her grandkids shocked Jamie. Bessie had turned down every offer to see them in their three years of life.

"And how is their daddy?"

Now that question floored her. Jamie had married some-one twice her age, and Bessie's small town mentality made her believe that the marriage did not consist of love.

"I don't know why you go and marry someone like that."

"Like what?" Jamie was instantly agitated. "Matt's a good man, and he loves his family . . . "

"Matt's a dirty ole man, that married you, trying to him young. You was just too stupid to see it!"

"So, you finally said it. You think he married his tramp. You know, you never respected me, and I swear I don't think you ever loved me, but I never thought you felt you raised a SLUT! And you know what else, MA MA; I'm glad you haven't been a part of my life since I got married, otherwise I wouldn't have a marriage right now. I'm leaving, you can die WITHOUT me!"

It was as though the bed ran to meet her fall. Tears soaked the sheets beneath her and carried her to sleep.

DAY TWO

Stupid chickens. The sun hadn't even risen yet. What were they cackling about? The taste of night lingered in Jamie's mouth. Stumbling to the bathroom, she realized she'd slept in the clothes she'd traveled in. A shower and a cup of coffee, then she would go home. At least, she thought, with Matt and the kids she'd be all right. There would be no more tears.

The toilet seat was cold and the coolness of it reminded Jamie of the time, her chubby little body slipped into the commode. Her mama had laughed so hard, she cried and farted all at the same time. She remembered as well, the care Bessie gave her when she realized falling into that big, white porcelain hell had really frightened her.

The warm water of the shower awakened Jamie's body. The memory of the toilet awakened her mind. She knew the right thing to do was to apologize to her Mama. As she wiped the water away, the quietness of the house worried her. Never did chickens crow, without Bessie banging pots in the kitchen. The towel fell to the floor and like someone crazed, Jamie ran through the house. Darkness blinded her. Furniture knocked her around. The living room. The pantry. The kitchen. NO MAMA. The TV room. Her bedroom. NO MAMA.

"MAMA . . . dear God, where is she?" Jamie felt her heart racing, her body gasping for her to breathe. Her body tightened in fear. All at once she heard the door slam and a light click on. It was Bessie. There Jamie stood, naked, with the most relieved, confused, stupid smile imaginable.

"I sure's hell hope that dumb smile and your naked body don't mean you snuck nobody in my house," Bessie laughed.

"You scared me Mama. Why didn't you wake me? I would've gotten the wood."

"You can't even get your own clothes. How in the hell you gon' handle fire wood!"

Jamie went back to her room and dressed. By the time, she returned to the living room, Bessie had gotten comfortable in her favorite chair. Jamie noticed how the chair wrapped itself around her, like a blanket. She also noticed how Bessie looked pale; the reddish glow just beneath her light brown skin was gone. The softness of her skin was now fragile and dry. Her body was tired, just there.

"Mama, you feel alright? You look tired." She stroked her mama's hair.

"I am tired. Guess I shoulda let you get the wood."

Jamie could see a look of what seemed to be love and fear in her mother's eyes. Was this the first time in more than a decade she would get a hint that, maybe, her mother did love her.

"Mama. I'm sorry about what happened last night. I do love you Mama. I want to be here for you."

Jamie held her mother's face and planted a kiss on her chin and then her forehead. Within her mother's eyes were tears. There they stayed. Bessie never let anyone see her cry.

"I heard you crying last night. So many other nights. Sometimes I knew it was cause of me . . . I'd just cry witcha." She pointed to the edge of the wall that led down the hall. "I'd put my head right there on the wall. I b'lieve sometimes you could make this whole house cry. Walls, windows, ghost and all." She smiled at Jamie, knowing how confused she must have been. "You wanna know why I never 'pologized, don't ya?" She raised Jamie's face so that she could see her eyes, and she knew that there would be no tears in them. When it came to sorrow, Jamie was much like her mother, her tears were shed privately.

"You had to know I hurt Mama . . . "

"You had to learn to stop crying and handle what come yo' way, even if it came from me."

Jamie stood and walked over to the fireplace. Minutes passed. With each second, came what she thought was an understanding of what Bessie had said to her. With each minute came more doubt. No woman could hurt a child, the way Jamie thought she'd been hurt and excuse it as a strength builder. It couldn't be that easy and Jamie wouldn't let it be.

"Jamie. You don't like me, do you?"

"No. From the time, I was old enough to figure things in my own mind. I thought you were mean, especially to me." Poking at the fire kept Jamie from seeing Bessie's face; still she could hear Bessie laugh. but she didn't turn around. She just poked at the laughter. Poked at all those tears. Poked at knowing not even death was going to bring them together.

"I always liked you," Bessie was still laughing. "You always was a determined l'il wench. Like the time my Mama spanked you 'bout that strawberry patch. 'Stay out it she said', in it you went, time-n-time again, whooping after whooping, 'til you was full. That was always you. No matter what. You had to get what you want."

Determination seemed like a strange thing to make someone laugh and Jamie didn't want to feel the moment for what it was. Instead she wanted to run. To be home holding her sons, loving her man, anywhere but here.

"I'm going for a drive Ma. You'll be okay 'til I get back, won't you?" She touched her mother's shoulder on the way out, not waiting for an answer.

Driving through Pelham was always funny to Jamie. This had to be the only place where people waved at whoever passed by. Most of the people Jamie grew up with had moved away. Most of the old ones she didn't remember. But, she waved as she drove, because this is Pelham and that was the thing to do. Looking up the road, she could see that the church on the hill, where Paula often sang, had a fresh coat of paint. To the left, in the same place stood Poitier's Grocery, and Jamie thought aloud, "and you could use some paint too." It was strange to Jamie how a town could sit seemingly untouched by time. Turning down a side street, she found herself sitting beside the graveyard where she'd seen the woman as a child. As though she wanted that woman to give her some answers she walked through the cemetery, reading headstones, smiling at flowers left by loved ones. There was a freshly dug grave and Jamie thought to leave before the service started. Laughing to herself she figured, "I better check it out. It's probably Mama's and Lord help who ever dug it, if it's not deep enough." As quickly as she thought it, she turned to walk back to the hole, then decided whoever the hole was dug for, was none of her business.

She drove down to Thomasville to pick up some things for the boys; back to Pelham to look around downtown and the Coca-Cola plant where her grandfather worked all his life. She loved pay day at the soda house. She and her grandfather would pick up his check, and a case of sodas, then head to the pantry store for two dozen fresh glazed donuts before going home. She thought about how sad she'd been because her grandparents died and she wasn't with them. In that respect, she was glad she'd be there for Bessie.

DAY TWO EVENING

Pulling up in the drive, Jamie could smell baked corn coming from the kitchen. "I don't know why this woman cooks like this. Must be a country thing." Jamie walked into the kitchen and placed the bags on the floor of the pantry.

"Mama," she rose from the pantry and walked over to the stove, where Bessie tended to her pots. "Mama, what's wrong?" Jamie took her mother's hand from the counter top, and the pots on the stove, and led Bessie to her chair. "Take it easy Mama. I can cook you know. Just rest. I'll finish in the kitchen."

Moments passed before they spoke to each other. Jamie placed the dished on the table and smiled at the sameness of the house. The walls held the same pictures. There next to the fireplace was the bullet hole, left from a discussion between her Aunt Jean and Uncle Walter, about Uncle Walter's infidelity. On the wall behind Mama's chair hung the photo of Bessie and Jamie, taken when she was two, just three days after her father was killed by a man in the Do Drop Inn. At Bessie's request, Jamie never talked about her father after that. Then Jamie noticed her mother. Bessie's eyes were fixed on her, yet they didn't seem to see her. The blankness of the stare angered Jamie. The look held nothing. The same nothing of affection Jamie felt Bessie had given her all her life.

"You wanna eat Mama?" Jamie turned away and stepped back into the kitchen.

"No. I don't. Come here."

She heard her mother, but suddenly like a hard-headed child she refused to move.

"I said come here, child, you in my house . . . "

" . . . and as long as I am I'll do like I'm told." Jamie decided to check her attitude and deal with the conversation as it came.

"You scared for me to die; but what you really scared of is you dying wit me." Bessie's eyes held that same empty look. "You figure I never loved ya, and maybe I didn't." Jamie could feel something; it must have been twisting at her guts because she began pulling on her shirt there, and fanning fiercely as if the temperature of her body was rising like a mad beast ravaging human flesh. Yet, she said nothing; instead she stared in her mother's eyes, coldly, unfeeling.

Bessie continued, "when I had you. I didn't want children. I didn't even want the husband I had. When he got killed I was stuck witcha. But I won't scared a day of my life. I had to take care of you."

Jamie smiled and turned off the lights before heading to her room. As she undressed, she decided she needed to have the last word. Walking back to the living room, where Bessie sat in the darkness, she touched her Mama's face and said, "I love you."

DAY THREE

Not even the crowing of the chickens woke Jamie this morning, but the unusual warmth of the sun in the winter did. Fighting the feeling to rise, Jamie assured herself she'd be safe in bed. Still the sun lured her eyes open. Seeing the sun through the bedroom window made her realize that a strange fear washed her insides. Slowly, she sat up in bed, watching, feeling as though the walls around her were experiencing the same fear. Her feet touched the ground. With each step was the fear of a last homecoming, and knowing of one's life in closing. Pushing aside the curtain that led to her Mama's room, she pushed aside the hate, the fear, the love she felt for her mother.

"Mama, good morning." Jamie fought to sound cheerful, she imagined the days romping through the park with her sons. "I'll fix breakfast okay? You want sausage or bacon?" She pulled her gently by the arm. "Come on Mama. We'll get dressed up like we used to for breakfast on the first Sunday."

"Jamie. STOP it! The number for Mason's is here on the night stand."

Jamie's mind raced. "Come on Mama. We don't need Mr. Mason. We can get dressed up for each other."

"Open the closet there child and push them boxes over there to the sitting room."

Jamie opened the closet. In it hung a red dress. A pair of black shoes lie on the floor. She could feel herself collapsing. Grabbing on to her thoughts, she remembered the night she gave birth to the boys. How thrilled she knew Matt would be when she delivered twins. How clever she had been to keep that secret from him.

"Mama did I ever tell you, I didn't tell Matt we were having twins. And how I cried like a baby. Mama . . . Mama . . . "

Then it hit her. From the way, her body nearly folded, it must have been a pain she'd never felt before. It hit her again and again and again.

"Jamie . . . you be careful on your drive home. I left you some sodas and chicken in the icebox. You be careful."

And it hit her. Anger pushed her to the head of the bed, where Bessie lay sleeping forever.

"YOU GET UP AND TELL ME YOU LOVE ME!" She pushed her Mama's still body. Shook her frantically. "YOU BETTER WAKE UP AND TELL ME YOU LOVE ME. I love you. Just say it. I love you. GET UP BESSIE. DAMN YOU. GET UP AND tell me you love me."

She didn't move. Jamie sat on the floor next to the bed, her mother's hand held to her heart, crying.

The sun always seemed to set slower in Georgia winters. It was the shadows cast by the setting sun, that told Jamie to call Mans's and Matt. Bessie seemed different. Not at peace. Not resting. But different. The blanket that draped her was her favorite. A pink one with red and yellow roses stitched in a hug bouquet in the middle. Jamie touched it as she walked out the room, closing the curtain behind her. Mama, she thought, liked her privacy.

DAY FOUR

"May the dust that covers this soul's body know that it is blessed with the soul of a child of God. Ashes to ashes. Dust to dust. This child begins eternal life with the Father, the Son and the Holy Spirit. Amen."

Jamie looked at the few faces that had come to say goodbye. How far removed they seemed from her. One by one they paid their respects and left. Alone with her Mama again, she knelt beside the grave and tossed in a pile of dirt with her hands.

"You couldn't even say you love me, so I'll always know you didn't. Unless. Unless you want to tell me now."

There was nothing. Of course, Jamie knew there wouldn't be. But she believed the dead could tell you what they wanted you to know, so maybe. Just maybe.

The road from the cemetery stretched itself out. Jamie was ready to go home to her boys and her husband. There were no tears to be wiped away and for the first time since she'd been back in Pelham. There were no childhood memories tapping her on the shoulder. As she applied the brakes for the stop sign, she reached into the bag of chicken, Bessie had fried for the trip home. A bone, or so she thought, pricked her finger. ripping the bag open, she found something that, although it should of, neither shocked nor thrilled her. A gold broach with pears and diamonds. her smile turned into a delirious cold laugh. She flung the car door open, and ran back to the uncovered hole that housed Bessie.

"Here. YOU TAKE IT. YOU DON'T LOVE ME. Remember. YOU DON'T LOVE ME!"

The broach landed snugly between the coffin and the dirt. Jamie settled back into the driver's seat and headed home.

The smell of Pelham had faded away. None of it mattered anymore. Not the church on the hill. Not gospel in the chicken coop. Not the field trips to the soda house. Not hearing Bessie say I love you.

Her boys met her at the door, as they always did. Their little arms squeezed her neck, ever so tightly.

A Look At Myself

"I can't believe you won't go out with him. The man is fine!"

"Fine is not everything. Besides I hear he's already in a relationship."

"Don't even try it. You're just too afraid to get with a good man because you've been with so many bad ones."

"You know, I could marry a prince, and you wouldn't be satisfied. Nag, nag, nag . . . "

"See what I mean? You settle for a prince, when you deserve a KING."

"JESUS . . . "

It was fright that broke the rhythm of conversation. Lisa and her, I can tell her anything, lie if I want to, call to cry, couldn't make a major decision without her friend Ruby; had walked up and down this mall more times than either of them could remember. Yet for the first time, this mall would be the sight of awakening realizations.

Lisa stood motionless, afraid to turn away from the vision in the storefront.

"I didn't see myself." Lisa stumbled for understanding of the words that fell from her mouth. "I looked, and at first I didn't see . . . I wasn't there."

Now Ruby figured Lisa was just tired. "Lisa be real. Your image is right there next to mine. You must've looked on a blink or something."

"Maybe. Probably," reasoned Lisa.

Ruby pulled Lisa away from her glass captor. Concerned but not worried; she did as anyone would have done faced with the possibility of insanity, began a new conversation.

"Come on," said Ruby. "Let's hit the food court."

The escalator ride up gave Lisa time to think about the image of her non-image. Was she really not there? Was it some type of supernatural warning to look at the way she was living her life. But Ruby was probably right. Lisa had looked on a blink and her mind took the opportunity to play jokes on her. So back to the business at hand, and just in time, she nearly fell from the bump as the escalator reached the third floor.

"LISA!" Ruby had that man alert tone in her voice. The tone that always reared its curious head when she thought it necessary to fix Lisa up. "Look at the sub counter. Now I can surely see you holding him. As a matter of fact, I can see me holding . . . "

"No, you don't. Every time we venture out you do this. NO MEN. Not for you. Not for me. Think food woman, food. Put your hormones in check."

"You know," observed Ruby. "You're the kind of thing that could ruin the most passionate of fantasies."

"Oh, please girl." Lisa's attention wandered from Ruby momentarily as she scanned the flashing menu board at Luigi's. She always ordered the same thing, so the scanning of the menu was basically a time stalling method. "What do you want?"

"If I told you, you'd make some off the wall remark about my sexual prowess. I'll settle for stromboli."

"One stromboli and one calzone please. And two large waters." While placing the order, Lisa glanced at her reflection in the metal siding on the cookie bar next door. Naturally, the image was somewhat distorted, but the true distortion was in Lisa's forlorn look of non-recognition. Could she not recognize the woman she saw?

"Lisa. Lisa." Ruby nudged. "Grab the tray. I'll get the napkins."

The two settled into extremely uncomfortable chairs that accompanied a wobbly table. Lisa laughed as Ruby noted her keen ability to find the funkiest tables, in the worst spots. She knew this, because Ruby continuously pointed it out.

"Where's your mind dreamer?"

Lisa hated being called dreamer. She would often share the opinion that the title meant she spent her time in imaginary worlds pretending to feel things that were non-existent.

"Don't call me that," scolded Lisa. "Rube, can I ask you something and get a serious answer?"

"Sure. What's on your mind? You still thinking about your image downstairs?"

"Yeah, I mean. It was just. I don't know . . . freaky. Like your cooking." Sure, the jab was unnecessary but Lisa couldn't help it; she'd been looking for a word to describe Ruby's attempts at culinary sufficiency for years.

"Oh. So, okay. You want a serious answer from me, but wanna put down my cooking."

"Okay. I'm sorry. It just popped out." Lisa kept laughing. "So. What did you want to ask me?"

Lisa wiped the cheese from her mouth and fingered the straw in the cup of water.

"You'd get a better reaction if you were doing that to a man." Ruby stopped Lisa's nervous hand from wiggling the straw. "Now. What's up?"

"How can everything be so sexual with you? I think you hide behind all that . . . "

"Is that the question you want a serious reply to?"

"No."

"And so?"

"You know how people say everyone has a twin some-where in the world? Think about it. If you were in this mall. And you saw you coming your way. Would you recognize yourself?"

It was certainly not the kind of question you'd expect to be asked. But still it was a question Ruby found difficult to deal with. Especially since the first answer to come to mind was NO.

E. Claudette Freeman

"I know it sounds crazy. I don't think I would know me. You know I think I would recognize some physical characteristics, but the person . . . I don't know."

Though listening Ruby found herself searching the faces of the crowd that surrounded them. What if? Could it be possible?

"Ruby. Ruby. You listening to me?"

Ruby turned her head slowly towards Lisa. Lisa's face was recognizable. But what about her own. It wasn't just the color of her eyes, the size of her nose, or the thickness of her lips. It was the character. The soul. The disappointment.

"I hear you. I want to tell you a story. Don't worry, I'm not going to change the subject. One day, I got home from work, dog-tired. I laid down for a few minutes to rest my eyes. Didn't fall asleep, just rested my eyes."

"And. Stay focused Ruby."

"Okay. I opened my eyes after about, maybe 10 minutes and when I rolled over; there was this person and the image of this little girl. They both looked like me. But I wasn't sure. Then after a few seconds they faded away. I sat up quickly, freaked out and tried to figure out what my head was doing. Then I realized I didn't see myself, but parts of me I'd lost. It's all about how we see ourselves."

Ruby pushed away the tray in front of her and looked around.

"You think other people think about things like this?" Lisa asked as she gathered up the trays and headed to the trash bins.

"I'm sure someone, somewhere does."

On the way down the escalator Ruby noticed her image in the mirror outside the photo studio. Yet she did not want to and quickly looked away. As her eyes moved away from the mirror, Lisa's eyes caught it. They stepped off the escalator and into a card shop.

"You know what? Some mornings, I look in the mirror. I dress up the skin, but I never really see me. Me, Lisa."

Lisa picked up a card, with a photo of an oily brown-skinned man, clad in black bikini briefs. She handed it to Ruby. "Here this looks about your speed."

The card was to lighten the moment, but Ruby was to intrigued in the thought that she didn't know who she was; not even that enticing portrait could break the spell.

"Sometimes I wonder what it would be like to be someone else. Aah, now this is interesting . . . " Ruby had discovered a box of dandy-candy lace panties. Lisa placed the box back on the shelf and they ventured back into the mall.

"I wonder what it would be like to be someone else too. But not just anybody. Specific people. Like my mother, Coretta Scott King, my child. But you know what? You know how people say black people wonder what it's like to be white. I never have. Being black is the one thing I always recognize about myself. It gives me a past. A meaning of sort."

"Somebody specific, huh?" Ruby thought for a moment. "I don't think about being somebody specific because I'm afraid that means I'm not happy as me, and I am." Ruby stopped and fixed her hair using the display case of a health food store as a mirror.

"Lisa, come here."

"What?"

"Look. It's two people who can't see themselves."

"You say that sarcastically, but I know you're serious." Lisa continued. "Look at us. Are we just combinations of our family and friends. When you look in a mirror, do you really see yourself? Or do you see what people tell you they see?"

Lisa turned to face Ruby, who stood stroking her face, staring at the image in the display. Cans of diet drink powder made the image look like a puzzle. Pieces not really in place. Some don't fit. We pound them, push, prod, curse and damn them until they fit. Pushing the uncomfortable pieces into others that

E. Claudette Freeman

had long ago settled. Never realizing that happiness of self may not mean using or even needing all the pieces. Ruby pulled Lisa towards the door that led to the parking lot.

"I think you never see yourself in a mirror, or anything that lends you your reflection."

"What?" Lisa was confused and she had to push Ruby into a further explanation.

"Lisa, we're always ourselves. The self is us. Understand. To see our image is to see what we want to be, or what we wanna see in our life. Kind of like seeing forward, not seeing present."

"I guess that can make sense," Lisa said.

"Listen Lisa. When you didn't see your image, it's because there is something you are not seeing in you."

Ruby picked up her pace for a moment and silence walked with them. Then they joked about who was to remember where they had parked.

"Don't tell me we're on the wrong side of the mall, Lisa."

"No silly, here's the car over here. What you said makes sense. When there's something wrong, we don't see a whole self."

"Something like that. Lisa, you just have to be smart enough to look at your life as closely as you look at that image. Just like you use make-up to correct flaws on your face, you have to use your mind to address what your image is showing you."

Lisa stuck the key in the lock of the passenger door slowly, noticing her image. Ruby stood next to her and likewise noticed the image.

"You know Rube. I am going to call John Leonard tonight. Maybe he is a good man. And I guess I do deserve a king."

Ruby rested her chin on Lisa's shoulder and smiled, knowing that Lisa must have seen something new in her image and knowing that something was much deeper than just a man.

Perhaps it was knowing she could see different selves each time she looked in the mirror. Maybe it was believing the images could improve the self she currently existed in, or even that self and the image of self could be recognizable even as a stranger on the street.

"And the man is fine Lisa. Let's go by his house." Ruby's face lit up as she hopped in to the front seat giddy from the adventure she began to cook up in her mind.

Lisa settled under the steering wheel.

"Hey, Lisa . . . "

"What?"

"Look in the mirror. Who do you see?"

"A great looking, intelligent woman, that knows she is that and so much more."

A comical, curious came upon Ruby's face. "All I see is a woman that truly needs this comb!"

"Ruby. You do know we are not children and we will not, I repeat, will not be randomly driving past a man's house."

Lisa turned the volume up on the radio, and raised her hand to Ruby's ravings and perfectly good reasons to be silly for the sake of setting up romance. The two bantered like hyped-up teenagers and each time Ruby got louder, Lisa turned up the radio's volume. The Ruby would listen for half a second as Lisa tried to assure her she was content as a woman in the current moment. She said she was better than good, and better than most.

"No, Ruby. Not listening. La, la, la, la – ain't nobody listening . . . "

KC's Gone Away

She peeped across the rusting metal fence that enclosed my family's piece of the neighborhood. Never speaking, she swung curiously on the open gate; then finally crept to the porch where I sat pretending to ignore her. She closed her eyes and rested against the trembling porch railing. The sun seemed to dance against her brown skin, highlighting wisps of curly hair on skinny yet muscular arms and a pair of tom-boy legs. Her rich black hair pulled tight into a pony tail hung just above her waist. She somehow reminded me of the black baby dolls at Grand-way Superstore.

"What you reading?" She asked, lightly touching the cover of "IF BEALE STREET COULD TALK".

"It's a book by James Baldwin. I've read it four times." It was the first time we'd looked at each other face to face.

Her eyes drew deep in questioning. "Why? Must be full of a lot of hard words."

"What's your name?" I asked, again pretending not to really be aware of her.

"Katrina Coles. You can call me KC. Your name is Tracy, isn't it?"

"Why ask if you already know?"

"Just being polite. Is that a hard book or what?" She closed her eyes to the sun again.

"No. I just like it. It's a love story. Want me to read it to you?"

"I don't care." She made herself more comfortable on the porch, moving in to the shade; looking for a spot where the heated cement porch wouldn't burn her thighs.

That summer, KC, the kids in the neighborhood and I did everything together. Like most brats on summer vacation, we played the old games like hopscotch, developed new ones, and challenged each other in our own summer Olympics. KC was the fastest runner. By September, she had developed the strongest pair of legs and was determined to be the star runner and jumper on the park's track team. And that whole summer KC would find her way onto our porch each time she saw me reading.

The sun-bathed brown girl that shared the words of Baldwin with me that hot summer is not the same creature that stumbled onto my path the other day. KC was gone. It was a startling reality. The beautiful girl with thick black hair and bracelet-graced wrists was now the type of person I made quick turns to avoid at traffic lights. God himself wanted me to see KC like this. To see the way the torture and rape of her life dressed her in death's clothes.

"Hey lady, let a man get a dollar for a burger. You can do that can't you."

She did look like a man. The long ponytail, made way for a scalp-close cut, and patches of scaling, pussing sores. Her muscular legs hid beneath scars. Her bony ankles strengthened by a pair of high-top sneakers, one with no strings. Except for the protruding belly that hung over the band on her shorts, she could have easily been mistaken for a man. And from her tone, talk and mannerisms, she had convinced herself that she was one.

The fact that she didn't recognize me was insignificant. Yet the figure of the man-woman before me brought a swelling in my throat, worsened by the sudden pains in the quickening breaths heaving from my chest.

"Come on KC, get in," I reached over to unlock the door. "I'll get you something to eat."

Scrambling to the passenger door, she spoke to a friend that only she could see. Not knowing the woman who had fallen into my path again, I knew it must have been the unseen friend that brought me to her recollection.

"You Tracy, huh? Girl, I don't usually look this bad. You know. It's . . . you know how it is."

I watched her knock dust from a tattered shirt. I saw her momentarily embarrassed by the dark sores that were scattered about her. I trembled at the sight of her trying to cover the scar on her neck, a scar that appeared to be from a bullet. Then I struggled to hold my quickening breaths at a normal rate, when she tried to pull her shirt over her pregnant belly.

"What you doing out here KC? Where you living?"

She looked away from me shyly, "I work out here, carry people grocery and stuff, please a man every now and then. Dudes always did like me cause I do them right."

"That sounds dangerous KC!"

She pounded her chest in her own self-victory. "Not for me, cause I pull up, things get to freaky. I pull up." She moved her arms and legs in a runner's fashion. "You remember, I was the fastest thing on the block. You married now?"

"Yes. Where's your family?"

She looked around the car, as though the door locks, the ashtrays, might as well have been her family. Then she cast her eyes out the window.

"They don't have too much to do with me, especially since the sores started showing up. My boyfriend shot me one time. You know about that? It was all in the papers and stuff, he caught me dancing with this guy. He in jail now. You know about that? Sometimes people buy me a beer or some, wine. Wild Irish Rose. Will I Run. You remember how I like to dance?"

"Yeah, you tried to teach me."

She laughed. And shook her head. So, I laughed too. Then I saw a tear fall from her reddened and swollen eyes.

"I sure hate you had to see me like this. I'm moving away soon. I'm gonna get better then come back. I'm still going to be a runner."

We turned into the parking lot of the grocery store. KC danced in her seat. I touched her shoulder softly. She pulled away. In my heart of hearts, I knew that it had been forever since anyone had touched her with good intentions. She was scared. I slowly reached my hand toward her stomach, when she did not pull away, I stroked it gently.

"I'm just glad I got a chance to see you again. I don't care how you look. I'm gonna give you my address and my phone number. You can come see me anytime you want to. And I'll take you home, so I'll know where you live and then I can come see you to."

Aisle by aisle, KC drifted between her version of her reality and the past she remembered. Sometimes I recognized her, sometimes I didn't care to. Home for KC was a rundown shack, surely condemned by the city. For what it was, it was clean and comfortable. We sat and shared a bag of chips, reminiscing. KC wondered aloud about the funny pains she'd been feeling in her stomach. I, finding it hard to hear that she was unaware of the child growing inside her, made her promise that she would go to a doctor; because I too had had those pains, and they would get worse in a couple of months. KC sat quietly for awhile, her head raised to the crumbling ceiling, eyes closed.

"I sure wished you had one of your books with you Tracy, you could read to me again."

I stood and gathered my purse from the floor, pulled my keys from my jeans and smiled. "Tell you what KC, I'll come by day after tomorrow and read for you. Deal?"

"Deal".

KC never came home the day I went by there. I looked for her on the corner where I had seen her that day. I tracked down her uncle, who not only hadn't seen her, but didn't want to. I told him she was pregnant. He told me, the Lord ought to do her and that baby a favor and take them both home.

Two months have passed and I still have not found KC. The shack she called home has been torn down. The broken recliner that once sat inside, now sits next to a sign that says NO TRESPASSING. Funny, I thought, staring at the sign. Is that the sign I gave KC, NO TRESPASSING? Reaching over to the bag on the front seat next to me, I pulled out a book, and stared at the cover. Then flipped to the introductory page of the novel. And it read, and so I read aloud, "If Beale Street Could Talk, it might tell the story of . . . "

The Slumber Party

The turquoise green cleaner formed puddles in the middle of the glass table. Puddles of memories. There in one of the drops, was the house we lived in on 177th street. When we moved into the faded blue house, Gabriela and her family were living in the white house next door. I remember thinking they must have been witches, because there was a little brick and glass house in front of theirs that held a little angel or something. Gabriela was my first friend on the block. Her dog snatched my favorite doll from my shaking hands one day. This plump lightly-tanned girl with curly, bright red hair gave it back to me. By the end of the day, she said I was her "mejor amigo en el mundo". For the next six months, we were best friends and enemies at least twice a day.

As I picked up the can of lemon-scented furniture polish, I recalled that we had lived in that suburb of international families for about a year, when Charde's folks moved in. She was a spitfire. Her fists took aim at the least offensive thing. She didn't like being teased, talked down to or even looked at in a strange fashion. Charde was a fighter. Charde, was a lonely, scared little girl. I always believed Charde fought people because her parents always fought. Her father once threw her mother, screaming and pleading from their front door. This was only after he held her suspended in mid-air, his blue-black hands squeezing her neck. He displayed her for the neighbors; his black and blue bruised woman.

Rose Lee came to Carol City two months after Charde. Thin as a toothpick, on windy days we would put her in the middle as we walked to school, afraid the wind would carry her away. She was always reading and talking. Rose Lee knew every kid in the neighborhood within three days maximum. Ms. Anderson, Rose Lee's mom was a civil rights activist. A lot of parents didn't like that so they wouldn't let their kids play with her. "My mama says you should know who you are and where you come from.

I come from Africa." Funny. To me, she had a northern accent, very proper and pronounced; like my cousins in Chicago. But I never disputed her heritage, though I often wondered if she disputed mine.

Shari Miller. I could never call her first name without her second name rolling from my tongue behind it. Shari Miller. See I still can't do it. Knocking the dust off the bookshelves, my mind searched for the period when we all, the five of us, came to be a group. I think we were about 10. Rose Lee, Charde, Gabriela and me, Daniella Reed, had been friends for two years then. Charde picked a fight with Shari Miller one day in the park. Surprised that she didn't run off crying at Charde's viciousness, I introduced myself and we all became buddies. Shari Miller had a gift for making things with her hands. She showed us how to paint t-shirts. The five of us had one just alike. Red roses on the front where we hoped our breast would bloom and our club name on the back, "The Fruit Loops Girls."

"The Fruit Loops Girls." Every Friday we would spend the night at each other's house. Turning the knob on the dishwasher, I laughed, Fruit Loops were still my favorite cereal. Once, the five us, got bold enough, to try chocolate milk with our cereal. Oh man, the stupid things we used to do. I still believe our slumber parties were the best. We'd cook. Color. Paint. Tell stories. Sing. See who could yell the loudest, of course, we always yelled into pillows so our parents wouldn't hear us. We would even have stupidest laugh contests.

One slumber party, I think we were 11, Shari Miller got her period. We all cried. So sure, that we had concocted something in the kitchen that made her bleed, we tried to hide it. But Ms. Anderson, decided to check on the reason for our quietness so early in the evening; and walked up on us as we taped Band-Aids across her vagina. I was in complete and utter shock when I learned that this was the period my mother often cursed. I started my period the following month. The others didn't start for another year. Once we all had it, we had new discussions and new things to experience. One Friday, we were about 13 or 14, all the moms got together to talk to us about sex. The following Monday, my mom took me to the doctor for birth control pills. I think it must have been the comment, "I can't wait to try that!"

The overnight rap sessions lasted throughout our high school years. Prom night, we had our slumber party at a hotel on the beach, complete with boyfriends. Our parents took turns calling every 10 minutes. Only one of us got to use any of the condoms we paid Andre to buy for us. The next special slumber party was the day after graduation. That's when we all announced which colleges we decided to go to and I announced that I was pregnant.

We had made a pact to leave on the same day; that way none of us would be left behind to cry lonely teardrops. I and Shari Miller, the University of Florida. Charde, Alabama A & M. Rose Lee, Fisk University. Gabriela, the United States Army. The last sleep over was on March 17th, the following year. The four of them were there the first time I took my son home. We nicknamed him Pigskin, because the nurses said at 10 pounds six ounces, he would surely play football.

Seven years have gone by since then. As I packed the last of Pigskin's shirts into his bag, I realized how crazy it was. A grown woman looking forward to a slumber party with other grown women. Careers. Families. Legal woes. Financial troubles. We needed this break. We needed to be the Fruit Loops Girls at least one more time. Pigskin was going away with his father, so I figured now was as good a time as any.

I worried about seeing Rose Lee most of all. For the last few years, I had seen and heard her quoted in the media. It was not her pro-blackness that bothered me; it was just the blacker she became the further apart she grew from Gabriela and me. Gabriela is Mexican. My mother is black, but my father is Dominican. It seemed to me in her quest to stay black, she forgot that she had friends who loved her, no matter where she came from.

Seven o'clock. Charde was the first one to arrive. The youthful and wiry looking woman, I last saw two years ago, no longer existed. In her place was a tired shell. Her face bore lines that stood out like scars. I held her in my arms briefly. I could feel her body trembling. Trembling. Trembling. But why?

Rose Lee was number two. I did expect the African garb, but the short, natural haircut, was a surprise, Rose Lee always loved her long hair. She still looked 18. But there was a stern tint to her face that I didn't recognize. Following Rose Lee was Shari Miller. She and I see each other often. She's a teacher at Pigskin's school. Over the last two years, she'd started lifting weights, and it was clear from her tight frame that her new healthy attitude was right for her.

It had been three and a half years since I had any personal contact with Rose Lee. When I hugged her I felt a little more at ease. There was, I was shocked to admit, a closeness in the embrace. As Charde and I set out the appetizers; Rose Lee poured the first round of drinks. A sort of fright filled me, as I watched Charde down a double shot of vodka, like it was nothing more than ice water. Moments later, the ever-late Gabriela arrived. And she looked good, slim waist, firm thighs, with the same curly uncontrollable hair. After hugging us all, inquiring about Pigskin's whereabouts and scanning the contents of the appetizers buffet, she laughed, "que paso . . . no fruit loops?!"

Memories, anecdotes, who's doing what, filled the first hour or so. Then, the devils hidden in the closets of our minds broke free. Shari Miller was telling the story of how I had been called to the school to discipline my son about his attitude, when Charde lashed out.

"Don't ever hit a child for no petty shit like that. How can you beat on your baby like that? What's wrong with you?"

I was shocked and scared. She seemed to be towering over me. Her long braids flying wildly as she flung her head in fury.

"Calm down Charde," Shari Miller urged. "She didn't beat on him. She just spanked him. That's all girl. Tap, tap. Spanked him. Though the way he hollered you would think she had abused him or . . . "

WHAP! The sentence did not complete itself, before Charde's hand landed against Shari Miller's face. She, Charde, was in tears. Her body shook violently. Rose Lee grabbed her, pressed her arms against her body trying to calm her down.

"It's not funny Shari. I don't mean to hurt my babies. They're all I got and I can't keep them. It's not funny Shari . . . it's not funny."

I stroked her arms as Rose Lee continued to hold her. There was an anxiety, a death in her eyes. She was ashamed. Afraid. Lost.

"You losing your kids Charde?" I asked, not sure if I was prepared to hear the answer.

She closed the eyes that showed her pain. "Not losing them Dani, giving them up. I beat them to show them I love them. But when I beat them, they hate me. I have to give them up before I kill them. I don't want them to hate me, like I did my father."

Rose Lee squeezed her, burying her face in her neck and I held them both. There we stood. This trio of tears. Charde reached out to Shari Miller, whose tears now soaked the back of my shirt.

"I'm so sorry Shari." She pushed past me and pulled Shari to her bosom.

"It's all right Charde" She tried to lighten the moment, "besides you've been wanting to hit me since our first encounter."

"I've never wanted to hit you. Not hit anybody Shari. It's just. It's all I know. I didn't want to hit you."

Gabriela pulled the two of them apart; resting Charde on the couch next to her. She pulled her soaked hands away from her face folding them safely in her lap. Like dominoes tilted, Shari Miller, Rose Lee and I, fell into various chairs. And Charde's body still shook.

"Who have you called Charde? Is someone already coming for the children?"

She shook her head slowly.

"You didn't call social services or HRS or anyone like that?"

She shook her head and exhaled hard.

"Then you will can no one. Shari, I know as a teacher, you're supposed to report things like this, but please . . . listen Charde I will take the kids and you will get help. Don't risk never seeing your babies again."

I looked at Shari Miller, there was look of confusion, concern, and yet relief. Though surprised, I was happy that Gabriela had offered her a sanctuary of sorts. Charde was quiet for a few moments, then slowly she raised her hand, gently stroking Gabriela's face and said okay. Rose Lee was furious.

"Don't sell out like that girl. You should make sure your kids are in a home with a black family. We put our children in other people's hands too much as it is; that's why they have no sense of self and culture."

"HOW DARE YOU!" I yelled. "How dare you stand your ass there and refer to Gabriela as 'other people'. She had the guts to make the offer before any of us did. Can you take them Miss strong and black? Can you?"

"That's not the point. If her kids went to foster care, more than likely they'll be placed in a black home, where they can identify. She could get her kids back from foster care with no problem . . . "

"I don't believe you. You of all people should know how devastating foster care could be for a black child, for any child." Shari Miller shook her head. "I believe enough in our friendship to jeopardize my job. At least with Gabi, they're with someone who loves their mother and them. That's what's right Rose Lee."

I walked toward the portable bar that sat calling me. Pouring the scotch in the glass, I felt a chill and a realization go through me.

"Would I qualify as a Black family Rose? Would I be good enough, since only half of me is black?" I raised my glass to Rose Lee.

"What does that mean?"

Gabriela rose slowly from the couch. Folding her arms across her chest, she stood so that her face was clearly visible to Rose Lee.

"I am 'other people' now? Or have I always been other people to you? For years. From kids, we have shared life. You were black then and we were inseparable. Are you blacker now? Is that why I am now 'other people'. No. I can't teach her children to be black, but it is not something you can do either. They were born black, I can only help them to understand what that means . . . "

"How in the hell do you know what it means? Just because you grew up with us, doesn't mean you're an authority on blackness."

"That's enough!" Shari Miller knocked a tray of sausage to the ground. She now stood inches from the ottoman that held Rose Lee. "You hypocritical, bourgeois, oh-so for my people wench. You would rather see those kids thrown aside for "the cause", than to know that they're in the bosom of love."

"You all don't understand. If we don't save our children . . . "

"Shut up Rose Lee," Charde buried her clenched fists in her thighs. "My babies are in a black family. What does it get them?

Beat. Beat and more beat. I don't want to lose my babies. This has nothing to do with black or white."

"Bull shit Charde" Shari Miller laughed.

"You see," I chimed in "Charde, Gabriela. It's all black or white. Sister Rose don't want know Latino or milked down Negro like me watching little black babies. She too 'afraid we still b'lieve in slavery. Ain't that right ma'am?"

"I should've never come here." Rose Lee snapped. I'm proud of who I am."

"And I am not Rose Lee? I am Gabriela, the Mexican. Of this I am most proud. I'm also proud and happy that I grew up around people, friends of different cultures, and I never knew what it was to be hated for color or race. Until now. And I would never think I would learn to be condemned like that, from someone I love as a friend." Gently she pulled Rose Lee away from the ottoman and kissed her on the cheek. Heading towards the kitchen, she stopped briefly near Charde, "if you wish not for me to take the kids then so be it. I cannot lie, I will not understand if you take them elsewhere. But I will still be here for you. If you all will forgive me, I cook when I feel like crying."

Kneeling at the gold-trimmed glass coffee table that sat in the middle of the room, I lit a cigarette. Shari Miller picked up the sausages and toothpicks that lay scattered about the floor. Charde looked puzzled, though I certainly could understand why. She extended a hand to me.

"May I have one please?"

I held the lighter steady and watched the tiny flame start to burn the tobacco.

"When did you start smoking?"

"Bad habit, I've picked up from Rod I guess."

Bitterness lingered in Rose Lee's voice.

Charde inquired, "who's Rod?"

"Rod is her latest mistake!" The tray of miss-arranged sausage crashed on the end table. I look, matter-of-factly at Shari Miller.

"My latest mistake. And so, what's really on your mind, Miss Too-cute-to-give-up-any?"

"Come on Dani," her smugness enraged me. "Part of the reason your son has such an attitude problem is because you always have some new man."

If I, if we were still kids, I'd have Charde whoop her ass right now. But I'm supposed to be an adult, so I will not do that - yet.

"I have had three steady relationships in the last five and a half years. None of them have ever spent the night in my house, never has my child awakened in the morning to find me gone. You, baby-doll, need to stop worrying about what you can't have."

For the first time that evening, a smile graced Charde's face. I heard Gabriela say something like Adios mio, no otra vez. Vindication was the veil over Rose Lee's face. I could hear her mind saying, 'aah, your turn.'

"And just what does that mean? Worrying about what I can't have?"

Charde spoke so quickly, it was hard to understand the words.

"Well you haven't had a boyfriend since high school!"

"I. I. Why do you say that?"

"Shari! You told us that a little while ago. Honestly speaking . . . " Rose Lee swirled the ice in her glass with her finger. "I've always thought you preferred women. The only boyfriend you've ever had is gay. Or maybe that just messed up your head. What'd you call me? Bourgeois. That's cool. Confused."

"You vicious bitches . . . "

"Hey, hey now. No one called you dirty names when you were in my business." Rose Lee brushed passed her, defiantly pausing, I guess to see if Shari Miller would make a move. She didn't. Gabriela's heavy sigh of relief washed over the room.

"What has become of us? We used to talk about everything. We would help each other unconditionally. Now. We accuse. We call names. We forgot, Rose Lee, where we came from."

Charde slowly doused the remnants of her cigarette in the ashtray. I did likewise.

"She's right. We planned our lives together." Charde looked at each of us. It was a look that called us all to judgement. "Shari wants a woman, fine. She's still been a good friend to me. Gabriela's not black. Fine. She cares enough about me to offer her hand in a time of need. Rose has let the cause taint her views, well, okay. Maybe it takes friends to make her vision clear again."

Rose Lee walked to the kitchen door where Gabriela stood quietly. Like all of us, she was wiping away the tears from her eyes. The walk was a slow one, like a child heading for a spanking.

"Gabi. I'm sorry . . . you have been one of the closest . . . " she grabbed her and held her tightly. "I'm sorry girl. My fight's not with you. I am sorry. Please . . . "

"Don't say it. You need never ask. I love you."

"You know what?" Shari Miller seemed to be laughing through the tears. "We have to be the most dysfunctional group of friends I've experienced to date."

The rest of the night was easier. We talked. Rose Lee explained why she had gotten so deeply into black liberation and civil rights. We kept working things through. We confessed. Cleaned within. Gabriela made cheesecake. From time to time one of us would break into tears. Then we'd all converge for a little hug therapy. I gave Charde the number to a counselor. She gave Gabi a list of things the kids liked and they worked out a visitation schedule. Gabi, I'm sure, still felt shafted by Rose Lee, and so, asked if she would bring by some books or games to help the kids learn about their heritage.

By the end of the night or start of the day, we were the fruit loop girls again. Shari Miller decided she wanted us to meet her friend. It seemed almost natural, the questioning. What does she look like? What does she do? Is she black? Does she have a brother? A straight brother? You know, as kids, we accept our friends for the good feelings we share. As adults, we choose our friends based on needs in our life. Aah, to be a kid again.

The next slumber party was a handful. Pigskin, Charde's three kids, and Gabi's two nieces. How did our mothers ever make it through the night?

My Piano Man

He followed a rhythm familiar only to his ear. Rapping, tapping, beating with the rhythm, his foot rose and fell in a steady manner; each time it hit the ground; I felt my heart crumble just a little more. When he played, there was something so engrossing about him. His music took him to another level, like a true singer grows ugly as the vocals rise, he grew more handsome. Sweat glistening on his brow, the muscles tightening in his arms as he swayed across those keys. Still, through everything, watching him, made me fall in love, deeper and deeper, year after year. My heart fell to his rhythm and even when he stomped all over me, all I could hear was the sweetest of melodies.

Time and time again, I followed him. Mombosa Bay, River Trek. Lilly's Place, Under the Tree. He never noticed me. You see, while he was magnified ten-fold in my eyes; I was but a speck of dust, made mud, by a puddle of water drifting from a warming glass. While I saw only him on stage attached to his true, true love; I'm sure my face was not recognizable as a love, but merely as another woman. The women were plentiful. They fought each other like drugged cats for his attention; on a bad night, he didn't give a damn. On those nights, he would hurt them, like he would hurt me. But they love him. I love him. Though sometimes I would tell myself, I don't love him as much now. I always realize that lie before it even clears my thoughts, I still . . . I still love him. So much a hoe, he should be permanently placed in somebody's garden, this I know . . . and this, I know, man, I still love him.

When I met him, he and his old band, were playing at a rustic joint in the black part of a central Florida town. He was average height, with solid muscles, hands that stayed warm and an unbelievable pair of eyes. Fancy brown, yet clear, like marbles. He told me the night I met him, that I was going to be crazy for him and he was going to love me crazy. I slapped him. But he

191

played that night and he constantly watched me. Watched me until I was uncomfortable. No one had ever seduced me with their eyes, and with fingers that never even touched my ashy brown self. I knew him two days before I packed up everything I had and followed him. From clubs with peanut shells for the floor to clubs in Philly; his fingers seduced me and kept me at his side.

Then it stopped. But I couldn't leave. I had to take care of him. Had to protect him from the throng of women that tried to steal his attention. Those women. They . . . they poured their heaping breasts into his mouth. But the flicking of his tongue against them was, is, prevented only by the skimpy material of their clothing. They, slide caves of sin and satin toward his warm hands. If not for the way his fingers were dancing across the keys; they would have danced in their moistness. They would slide wicked little phone numbers down his shirt, and I'd collect them from the floor as he undressed under the rising sun.

"Baby what are those marks all on your neck and back," I asked him, more out of concern than suspicion.

"Played outside tonight woman. They aren't anything." He never even looked like the lie bothered him.

"Well, I'd better put some alcohol on them, make sure they don't get infected." *And hope that alcohol burns the hell out of your cheating ass too.*

"You sure do take care of me sugar. What'd you do all night?" *Well, I thought, somebody really must care about you.*

"I didn't do anything." *Nothing 'but watch you let them sluts rub all over you, like you some damned genie in a bottle.* "I watched a couple of movies, that's about it."

"You should find yourself something to do when I'm playing. You're going to grow old sitting around waiting for me to come home." *Not hardly sweetie, not hardly.*

"What am I supposed to do? You told me I'm not allowed at the clubs when you're playing. I'm not allowed at the clubs when you're not playing, and you don't like any of my friends, because they're not married. What am I supposed to do?" *If you must know, I do what I want, I spend time with you.*

He, got into a hell of a fight one night; because one of them, was actually a he, and he had lured him into the corner. I watched with tears soaking my faith as he rubbed with such tenderness the length of her-him. Until he realized, that length, was more than even he could offer. I watched with laughter blowing the tears from my face, when she-he knocked him unconscious to the floor. Then . . . he played the blues. Slow. Deliberate. Funky. Mournful. He played the sho'nuff blues. And I don't know why. I took the time to love my man so sweetly before he headed out the door.

"Oh baby, how you do me. Uhm, your fingers make me trill like high notes on a scale." *So why do you make them scream too? Can't you be happy with this thing, baby, can't you?*

"Is it mine baby?"

"Yes." *But you don't want it.*

"Is it what you want baby?"

"Ooh yes baby, don't take it from me." *Especially to give to somebody else. Stop doing that to me.*

"You want some more baby?"

"Yes. Baaaaby."

"Can you handle it baby?"

"Uhm hum." *Not knowing you giving it to everybody else, no, I can't handle it.*

"There you go girl. Damn, do it sugar, come on, yeah, that's it, that's it, girl the way you do me. You're like poison girl."

"I'm going to take you there baby. Let me take you there." *I got some poison for you. When I get through with you tonight, you won't be able to pee out of this thing.*

"Ease up sugar, you're gonna hurt yourself."

"Not hardly baby. Just don't let me go, all right. Can you do that? Hhm, can you hold me?" *Sure, you can, you're an expert at holding women.*

"Awhwh, girl, you gotta stop baby, I'll be late."

"Don't push me off like that. I gotta couple of more to get." *Don't be trying to take my feel good to the next woman, what the hell's wrong with you.*

But he was playing the blues. I was hearing my blues. I told him all the right things before he left home, didn't I? How every time he played my song, I had to dwell within myself and imagine his fingers playing my favorite song. How if he wanted to he could call me the names of the girls that played his horn while he tinkled his keys. I guess I didn't tell him. But I know I did, right about the time he told me I was trying to kill him, with my, well you know.

He said, "When were you at the club baby?"

And I said, "Every damned night sugar. Now, do you love me?"

I heard the door close soundly behind him. I guess tonight he's playing the blues but I want to jam. While he pounded on my heart with that foot of his; I stretched my long, dark self across the dance floor. His hands found themselves touching various parts of my body. I started scatting my way back to me. He, whispered dangerous lies of love in my ear. I scatted, scatted, scatted. More bullshit. Then he, finally looked up at me with him. And he, was playing that crazy jazz. He wanted me to hear a love call? I wanted to scat my back to home. Man, he was hurting me -- and I heard those keys calling me, but my scatting was louder than all of that. It was my song. My tune . . . you watch me sing this time.

They tapped their hussy-polished fingers across his chest. Like Betty Carter, I scatted. They, accompanied his jazz with warm vocals whispered in his ear by tongues lingering in seduction. I pulled him close to me.

"You move really nice brother. You don't mind me dancing in your arms like this, do you?"

"You can dance with me anyway you want to. What's your name?"

"Mystery."

"Mystery?"

"Yeah, you like mysteries brother? They're always such fun to figure out."

Like Nancy Wilson, full of fire, I scatted. They, ah, they shook the smoke away from 'his woman' with elusive, wide-butt, plenty-titty and little-brained bodies. I hear Ella saying, I dropped it, I dropped it. I crushed his empty heart on that pea-nut-shell covered floor, where I found his . . . man, I love him.

But you know he always came home without them. For the most part anyway. Their numbers would fall out of his shirts, when I hung them up, when I washed them, when I took them to the dry cleaners.

"This number fell out your shirt baby. Is it important?" *Important or not, you won't get it again.*

"Some guy, wants me to play at his club party." *Damn, how can he lie like it's the truth.*

"Baby, I don't think you should play there."

"Why's that?" *You're not even going to get nervous are you. Oh see, now this is pissing me off.*

"Because he wrote the number in lipstick darling. You sure he's not trying to tell you something." *You sure I'm not trying to tell you something.* He didn't even flinch. I must really be that stupid. He didn't even flinch. It doesn't even bother this nig-ger, knowing I found some wench's number written in lipstick, in the shirt, I'm standing up here laundering. He doesn't even flinch about it.

"Baby, you sure have one wild imagination."

"Hhm. That may be so darling, but in my imagination, a number written in lipstick is troubling." *Now, don't flinch.*

"What are you saying?" *Now that's a stupid question.*

"Now that's a stupid question. What am I baby, stupid? No, I can't be. I'm a college-educated, hard-working woman, that can run circles around your bench-sitting ass. You stand there and don't even flinch about telling me some half-assed lie. Ain't no joker in Dixie, gave you a phone number written in lipstick."

"It happens baby. You know that. Why you taking this to this level?"

"You've been playing me like you play that piano. I'm not that easy under your fingers anymore. Do you even feel bad lying to me?"

"Did you feel bad screwing up on that dudein the club tonight?"

"Not half as bad as I did watching them all over you."

"It's just part of the game girl, don't start this."

"You know I love you." *And I hate myself for it. I still love you more than anything in this life.*

This time there were no numbers in his shirt. "Baby," he said, "the answer is yes."

"Yes?"

"You asked me if I loved you?"

"Baby. That was days ago; it took you that long to think about it?"

"It took you that long to hear it." *Damn, he's good.*

And I scatted while he played his jazz on me. And maybe that number that fell from his pants, is really not a number at all. Ba dwee da dwee da, shoobie dobe dwee da . . . .

Moonshine Run

I ain't never seen four boys so outta breath in all m'years. They been runnin' that there moonshine through Devil's Field for 'most of da year now. Blasted fools. Damn police gon" hang 'em jus' as sho as they stupid. Look at 'em. Justa huffin' and puffin' and cuttin' da fool.

"Where Jabbo y'all? We swift-footed him again huh?"

"He gon" get us caught yet, man. We gon" have to leave him home next time. Devil's Field hard 'nough to run through as it is."

Jabbo. That damn boy outgrew his clothes and his senses all in one summer. He named after his daddy Jasper B. Bollin. The "B" don' stand for nothing. Leas' nothin' he could recall. Jabbo. Pooty. Walker and Chief. James Addie tol' 'em they could make mo money haulin' moonshine cross the woods, thenthey could workin' the fields. Sho he was right. Reckon he didn' tell em they was gon' get chased down like opossums, an' called to answer come Jud'ment Day.

"Man ... man ... I don' ... y'all keep on ... leavin' me ... I could get los' in there!"

"Damn Pooty man, you smell worse than a outhouse. You cain't run without cuttin' gas?"

"Shut up y'all. I cain't hep it. Ya know how I get, when I get excited. Lees I can keep up. Jes gimme ma money so we can split up, Chief."

"Here. Ya ain't gon" have it when I see ya tonight. Lose it on them squares on the ground all the time."

"Man, it's my money. Spen' it how I wanna."

"Chief com' on, we'll walk back together. That way, if we get stopped by the man. We can vouch for each other. Later Jabbo. Pooty."

Chief. He's the youngest of the bunch. Smart boy. School won' enough for 'im. He jes decided he won' goin' no mo. Po mama gave up on 'im. Tol' me theother day he wants to get married. All a 17, and he is wantin' a wife. Says he got someone in mind too. I sees him watching Abigail Barnes all the time. She switch them ole big hips extra hard every time she seems him stretchin' his eyes. Lord knows he can stretch 'em too. They gon'' spread so withe one day, they gon'' personally meet his ears. I swears they is.

But anyways. Abigail sees him and she be trying to switch and walk slow all at the same time. Knowing full well ya cain't do both. Least I ain't never seen a woman do it. And I'se been watchin' tail a long time. Chief run behind her like a dog chasing a rabbit. Picks wildflowers outta my garden for her. Buys her candy and stuff. Tries to give her money too. She won' take it tho'. Says her hands cain't spend no moonshine money. Whatever she' buy, she say, "would smell like that ole rottin' liquor."

She ain't but 15. But she mo mature than most of the grown women around here. Been runnin' a house since her mammy died. She won't but eight. Her and her daddy been taking care of each other since then. He had to comb hair, teach her 'bout the woman process and all. All by himself. I b'lieve he gon'' lose his right mind, once he find out Chief smellin' his gal's juice.

"Gail. When you gon' tell your daddy, I want you."

"My daddy don't need to know nothin' 'bout you. Reckons I ought to want you first."

"What's it gotta be Abigail Barnes? Anythang girl. I been saving my money. So ain't no worries. I'm gone' marry ya, and put some real hips on ya. My sons need to come from a woman like you."

"You been running through Devil's Field so long, you've out run yo senses and yo complete mind. Do I look like I wanna have yo children? You sho'll insists on a lot for a man ain't asked for a girl to escort you properly."

"Look girl. I don' want you for no girlfriend, I want you for my wife. Why yo head so hard?

"Chief. Why they call you out your given name?"

"Cause I don't like it."

"What is it?"

"Don' b'lieve you need to know."

"A girl ought to know what name her suppose husband to be come from the hole with."

"I ain't from no dark hole. Always was light 'round me. Still is. That's why you go to smiling evr'y time you see me."

"Hush lying. I do no such a thang. If I smile, it's cause life is good."

"It's cause I make you feel good. I know it. Johnny Love Turner."

"What's that?"

"The name you gon" take on as my wife."

"Folks say you part Indian."

"I is. My granddaddy on my momma side and my daddy . . . Cherokee."

"So,they calls you Chief. I see now why you sport such nice hair. Is it soft?"

"I'll let you touch it. But you gotta promise me you'll go walking with me tonight."

"Surely yo hair ain't so soft as my company would be Chief."

"You like to make me chase you, that's fine. Cause that's what I like 'bout ya. Hard head. Soft behind."

"Chief you keep your hands to yourself. I cain't go home smellin' like liquor. Silly child."

"You gone be my wife. When am I supposed to touch ya?"

"Ya ain't. Chief, why you runnin' shine? Seems to me any man wanna be a daddy ought to care 'bout other babies not getting' what they need cause they daddy spendin' money on moonshine."

"It's good money, Gail and it's easy. It ain't like I'm killing nobody."

"Johnny Love Turner, stop holdin' yo eyes closed. Shine ain't nothin' but poison, it eats folks' insides like an ole filthy tapeworm, suck the life right from ya. And you just about done killed yo po mama. I sees her in the store and ask 'bout ya. She just look sad and go to crying. Ya killing her wit' worry alone. And I worry 'bout you too."

"Gail . . . "

"Gone' way now, 'fore my daddy see you. He ain't got no respect for ya, selling shine and all. I'll see you tomorrow. Maybe we can go for ice cream."

"I love you Abigail. Hope you say I do soon. My heart be hurtin' all the time, and parts o' me ache for ya like they don't ache for nobody else."

"I know you do. And I will soon. Soon as you stop runnin' shine."

Them was some cussin' son of a guns, when Chief tol' 'em this was gon" be his last run. Walker pulled a knife on him. If Jabbo hadna hit him he mighta killed Chief. Pooty got real nervous. Now, I don't recollect the boy to well. But I does know, you cain't trust a animal pacing when there ain't no cage. Too nervous he was and I tol' Chief to keep an extra set a eyes on 'im.

It comes time for 'em to make that there run. Right 'fore sundown. Walker come over and po'd me a shot off the top like always. Didn' do much talkin' tho'. That was sho strange. Him, Chief and Jabbo stood 'round that stolen car, for 'bout an hour. Finally, they sees Pooty coming up Creek Road. I hear Chief tell Walker and Jabbo to leave, and they'll make the run shortly after 'leven. And he tell 'em don' spare the word to Pooty, "I smell perfume on a trapped skunk."

I reckons Chief figyad if Pooty was playin' best dollar out, he was gone' have to go to the other side of the field; and well by the time him, Jabbo and Walker got there, Pooty would be makin' his report. Chief come sit on the porch wit me. Us watch

201

Pooty. He gotta walkin' real slow after Jabbo and Walker run pass him.

"Mr. Nathan, I feels a storm blowin' in. Yessir, I sho do."

"Must be the Indian in ya. Yo Pa was the same way, feel the weather change."

"Yessir, I recall. Pooty pacing mighty low and slow, don't ya thank?"

"I tol' ya 'bout that extra set a eyes. Cain't negotiate with friendship when ya runnin' behind money."

"Sir?"

"Ya hears me Chief. Jus' pay 'tention to yo self. Ain't no such a thang as a friend when ya doing wrong for money."

Seems like it took Pooty twenty years to reach the house, look like he aged as much likewise. Chief talked him up good. I smelled Pooty's nerves up on the porch. Chief didn' say nary a word 'bout it and didn' mention the run either. When he come back up on the porch, Chief say he tol' Pooty, they was gone meet back here to talk 'bout da next run. And he told me he need me to do him a favor. Tol' me to pick them up in ma truck 'bout quarter to 12 by Hands Road. Seems he figyad out Pooty was gon" get mo money to fix it so a bootlegger could snatch the shine and take it cross the state line. Them bootleggers got after them once befo', shot Chief in the arm. Damn sho did.

Few minutes 'fore eight, Chief run off to meet Abigail. I knows he had to marry her. I mention her name and that damn boy couldn't 'member his. I tol' em, he was gone have to do some quick talkin' to get Barnes to give him his baby. Chief laugh, "Mr. Nathan," he says, "don' ya know if Gail wantsta marry me, her daddy cain't stop her." Sho he was right. Lil Abigail had a way with her daddy. And with Chief too.

"You late Johnny Love Turner."

"You gon' call me that every time ya mad at me for our lives?"

"Way I sees it. If I mad at ya, you'd better be glad I calls ya anythang polite."

"I'm gon" put ma arms 'round you Abigail Barnes and kiss you."

"You ain't 'posed to tell me it, fool. You 'posed to jes do it."

"If I jes did it, you'd more than likely hit me."

"I'se still gon" hit ya. What kinda girl ya reckons I am?"

"One that would send a boy to a crazy house. I ain' gon" kiss you then."

"Then I'll jes have to kiss you."

"Damn, Abigail. You been sharing those lips wit somebody else ain't ya?"

"Some thangs jes come natur'l. Like the way yo hands keep findin' my behind. Now move 'em. Fresh self."

"Gail. I love you."

"I keeps tellin' you I know that. Oh. Alright Chief. I loves ya back. Now you kiss me."

"You sho?"

"Yes."

"I do likes the way you feel on my body Abigail. I cain't wait 'til we married. Can I tell ya daddy yet?"

"I tol' him. But I tol' 'im I won't gon" marry you, 'til you stop runnin' that moonshine. You ain't a dranker are ya?

"No. You knows that Abigail. Where ya get a name like Abigail?"

"From my momma. She named me after some lady that taught her how to read and stuff."

"I've see ya naked befo' Abigail. Course I'se pretty sho, I'd like you better naked now."

"Johnny Love Turner you stop lying! I've never shown you my naked body!"

"Well now, I didn' say you did. You don't remember, but I used to stay at y'all house sometimes when my ma worked late. Evr'y time yo mama bathe ya; you'd run 'round the house naked. You gon" do that when we gets married??"

"I don't see why not."

"Gail, are you a virgin?"

"Are you?"

"You don't ask a man that question."

"You asked me. You wanna make love to me Chief?"

"I sho do. I cain't even tell ya how much."

"Do you know how to?"

"I guess so."

"You better know so 'fore we get married. You hear? I gotta go. You be careful tonight."

"What?"

"Jabbo tol' me. I ain't gon" say nothin'. Don't fret."

"I'll knock on yo window when we gets back."

"Fool. My daddy'll kill you for sho. I'll see you on my way to school in the mornin'."

"Gail. Can I leas' touch it? Jes once?"

"Don' do you no good to touch what you cain't get Mr. Turner. Now bye and please pray and be careful."

'Bout quarter to 'leven, they all showed up. Pooty was first. Trouble usually come early. Then Jabbo, Chief and Walker. Pooty was still nervous. Chief kep' smilin' at 'im. Walker kep' talkin' to him 'bout nothin' really. Jabbo kep' movin' way from 'im. Pooty jes kep' on watching Chief. Chief jes kep' on smilin'.

"Pooty we gon" take the car back. A storm coming in. Ain't no sense in runnin in dis kind a weather coming. We'll drop you home on the way, and Jabbo too. Walker and me'll run back."

"Man, James Addie gon" be mad."

"He ain't. Walker don' talk to him."

Leven thurty, I pulls off the side of Hands Road, not a spit from Jabbo's house. He jump in the back and laid down. Ten minutes later, Chief and Walker come runnin' up the road. They took me home, loadedthe boxes and headed off through Devil's Field. Them clouds moved in quick. Chief was right, a storm was coming. A weather storm and a man storm too. I'se gon" say an extra prayer for them tonight, that's what I tol' maself.

'Bout twelve thurty, Jabbo pull up in the truck. He say Chief and Walker hung back. Seems they saw Pooty talkin' to some folks that had shot afta them once befo'. Jabbo and I got skeered. It was 'bout an hour later when we hyeard em coming', but them steps coming' through the woods sounded awfully funny. Chief was carrying Walker, the best he could anyhow. Walker was taller and bigger than him.

He says Walker's tempa got the best of him. 'Fore he could stop 'em Walker had run up to Pooty and started whoopin' on him. Then the folks he was wit' started shootin' and they hauled tail. Chief say they was halfway back when Walker hit the ground. Look like he caught a bullet. Chief say he couldn't tellwhere. 'Course with the rain pourin' in buckets and all that mud, I 'magine not.

We got him on in the house and cleaned him up. He took a bullet in the gut, but hell by the time the sun come up, he had come to and was cussin' up a storm. Abigail Barnes come runnin' up, yelling for Chief. She say they caught Pooty in Lockersville just as they crossed the state line. His daddy went by Barnes' house to borrow money to bail 'im out. Chief say his mind told him to give his daddy the money. Walker said his mind tol' him to kill him.

"I'll walk you to school Abigail. Don't want you to be late."

"You been quiet for awhile now Chief. Pooty troublin' ya?"

"Yeah. I never expected he'd do something like that. We all grew up together, when I got shot he drug me up to the hospital. He was wrong Gail. I just cain't figya it out."

"Chief. My daddy always say if you gon" do wrong, do it by yoself."

"Why's that?"

"Cause ya cain't trust nobody who gone do wrong witcha. That's why I don't let you do wrong with me."

"Last night was my last time. James Addie won't happy, but I tol' him, I can keep ma mouth shut, he knows I can. Way I see it, y'ain't got no reason notta marry me now."

"How you plan on taking care of me with no job, I got a mind to finish school ya know."

"You are . . . I swear sometime I could put you cross my knee and . . . "

"Watch your thoughts Johnny Love Turner. How you plan to take care of me?"

"Me and Mr. Nathan gone start farming his orchards. We figya we might open a fruit stand down by the end of his acres, by the main highway."

"I reckon ya do know whatcha doing. You got a good head for the wrong kinda business, maybe it works alright for the right kind of business."

"Hey Abigail, how long it gon" take to get a license for marriage."

"I ain't to sure. How come ya want to get married? And why me?"

"Cause a man needs a woman, my daddy always said that. He got killed runnin' shine ya know. And just like runnin' moonshine, marrying you, fills my need for excitement."

"If I marry ya, I best be all the woman excitement ya need. I told daddy ya coming for dinner tonight. And I asked yo mama to come too. My daddy less likely to kill you in front o' ya mama. You gon' kiss me goodbye?"

"Naw. I figya'd you'd just kiss me. I love you Gail."

"I know you do. And I loves you even mo wit' no moonshine runs."

"Abigail. You can cook cain't ya?"

A Conversation With Vinnette

The newspaper clipping was vague. I read it repeatedly thinking there needed to be more. I would wait until tomorrow surely by then there would be a full obituary or at least a review of a life so pivotal in black theater. Theater period, though many would relegate her to black theater as though that was a horrible thing. For me black theater has always been what theater could be if it were not afraid of revealing life. Still, as I read the clipping announcing Vinnette Carroll's death and emphasizing that at her request there would be no memorial service, I found myself crying.

I am not at all impressed by one's star power and neither do I live vicariously through the lives of entertainers. I was crying because I realized that my brief encounter with Vinnette had a God-ordained purpose and I feared I had not acted on it properly. I had the honor of meeting Vinnette some years before her purpose in my life would manifest. A director and a small group of theater lovers had gathered in the lobby of her black box theater. It was to me an intriguing place – an old church renovated into a theater. It had a charm and personality as engaging and intimidating as Vinnette. That night we would read the words of Ntozake Shange's play "Spell #7". The director hoping to convince her that this was the one to do. Short on actors in the group, I was coaxed into reading one of the parts. Uncomfortable in this role, my voice was low and slightly shaky.

"Darling," Vinnette rested her sturdy brown fingers on the side of her face. "Don't you understand what is happening in this piece? Never, never simply read the words. You must experience them."

"Yes ma'am," I said amazed that I was being scolded by Vinnette.

"What – what is your name?" She smiled when she asked.

"It's Claudette." I replied, smiling back in her direction. In a strange way, I think she saw something in me and she was determined to draw it out.

"Claudette, do you like this author's work? Are you familiar with it at all?" She wanted to gauge my literary knowledge. I wanted not to be made a fool of. "Yes ma'am. I actually did an artist residency with her last year."

"Then don't disrespect her by not allowing yourself to feel her words. You are a woman. This is about everything that women experience. I need to hear in what you read that you know that experience. Do you understand?"

I understood. I understood not only the words in the Shange piece, but I understood the essence in the advice that she'd cast my way. Shange had given a similar piece of advice during our summer residency, and I adopted it as one of my writing mantras. She said every word you write should breathe, live and move. It had to have been four or five years later before Vinnette and I would meet again. An opportunity to do some public relations work for a play she was mounting allowed our paths to cross again. She said my name was familiar to her, but my face wasn't. I explained that I had cut off my hair to go natural since our first meeting. I also reminded her about the reading.

"You, you angel, are not an actor." She yelled a direction across the theater before I could answer. "I think you are a writer – I see it in the way you watch what's happening on the stage. Are you a writer?"

"Yes ma'am. I am."

"Come. Come site down here and next to me writer. I want to hear what you write." While we talked, she would yell at dancers, yell at actors and ask if they were serious about their craft or just there to get a paycheck. She cut to the core of one actress, who must have exuded more arrogance than talent for Vinnette's liking.

"You enter like you are a star. Everyone wants to be a star. The thing, darling, that you forget is that even the brightest stars fall from the sky."

She would grow quickly livid when actors had not captured lines and changes in the script; although she would, I was told, at times, change the script daily. She would ask the same question repeatedly. Finally, she explained she was being conquered by age and would forget some answers as quickly as she learned them. That was the reason for the daily changing of the script, I assumed. That and the strange fact that she was turning the one-woman piece Pretty Fire into a multi-cast production complete with musicians, dancers and singers. It was wild! It was a good show.

"Angel," she summoned me to stand next to her. "Help me up from this chair darling. My cane has fallen there." As I helped her steady herself, I bent to retrieve the cane. "You must come to my home and bring me what you write."

I'm not sure what I felt at that moment. I was thrilled. I was thrown off by the gasps from two of the actors who overheard the invitation. Vinnette apparently invited few into her private space. For me, the excitement was now mixed with anxiety. Was I being invited as an angel she found interesting or as the subject of a script idea she was building in her creative spirit? Two days later, with my literary portfolio neatly packaged and ready for a professional presentation I pulled into her driveway. She pushed her front door open with a wide smile beneath her gray, uncombed hair.

"You found your way," she laughed. "I was worried that I steered you improperly. What kind of car is that darling?"

I glanced back at my car observing it sorely needed washing. "It's a Toyota Corolla."

"I have a fascination with cars, you know?" She seemed to be quite attracted to this car; which amazed me. "Come, come in, and sit down with me. Do you have time this evening?"

"Yes, ma'am I can stay as long as you'd like. Here, this is my portfolio."

As she slowly flipped through the pages, rising at one point to find her "better glasses", I took in this home that spoke of the things that were clearly a part of her. The art work, the church pew that sat against the wall just inside her living room, the way the kitchen, dining area and living area all were applauded by a stunning view of the lake – it was clear – at least to me that careful planning had gone into this home.

We talked until the sun set, and the house grew dark. She didn't seem to notice that only the light from the TV illuminated the room until I said something. We talked how about those intimidated by your gift will seek to quiet your fire. We talked about abstract things like never allowing actors to tell a character what to do; how she believed her former maid was stealing from her and how writers must be careful about living too long within their own minds.

As I read the small article again, I remembered that feeling of awe when I walked into the church she'd transformed into a theatre. I felt at home there, like the walls knew every word I longed to write. I wondered if it was that same feeling that beckoned her to call that old church in downtown Fort Lauderdale her space. I read the small article announcing her death, and committed to write every word my soul could birth, as I heard her voice, boom - as it did - the most profound question she had asked in the three times we'd encountered each other. "Tell me angel, why do you have such talent – but - no one has seen it?"

I'm sure glad you did – Vinnette Justine Carroll.

ABOUT THE AUTHOR

E. Claudette Freeman spent some 24 years in radio in South Florida, before launching into literary coaching, editing, and commissioned stage/film works.

Freeman's honors include placing for two consecutive years in the Quest Theatre of West Palm Beach Loften Mitchell New Play-wrights' Festival, being a featured reader in the Miami Book Fair International's WRITE IN OUR MIDST PROGRAM, being chosen as an apprentice to famed African-American author Ntozake Shange, during the Atlantic Center For The Arts Masters Residency Program, co-authoring (with the late Bhetty Waldron) the touring production of CHARCOAL SKETCHES, a play based on the lives of Zora Neale Hurston, Augusta Savage and Mary McLeod Bethune and being commissioned to author a Black history production FROM THE PORCH starring Danny Glover by the Miami Sports and Exhibition Authority. Her worked has been staged in Miami, FL; Delray Beach, FL, Richmond, VA and Memphis, TN.

She is the author of the collection of short stories: **PIECES AND ME**; three invigorating and engaging devotional/essay jour-nals **THE MORNING HOUR: ARISE, WRITE, RELEASE; FAB-ULOUS YOU: POWER NUGGETS FOR THE MOMENT** and **IF I WRITE IT, IT CAN HEAL**. She is also the author of three collec-tions of a trio of journals: **ENDURING WOMAN JOURNAL COL-LECTION, KEEPSAKE POWER JOURNAL COLLECTION** and the **WRITER'S MUSE JOURNAL COLLECTION**. Freeman is also the author of **WHEN I DANCED WITH GOD**, recounting spiritual-in-fused and inspired dreams and their interpretations. Freeman lives in South Florida with her son Isaiah Langston-Michael Freeman.